The Apple Picker

Morag McKinlay

The Pentland Press Limited
Edinburgh • Cambridge • Durham • USA

First published in 1996 by
The Pentland Press Ltd.
1 Hutton Close
South Church
Bishop Auckland
Durham

British Library Cataloguing in Publication Data.
A Catalogue record for this book is available
from the British Library.

ISBN 1 85821 416 5

Typeset by CBS, Felixstowe, Suffolk
Printed and bound by Antony Rowe Ltd., Chippenham

With love and admiration, I dedicate
this book to mamma, Alice Baird,
whose memory is a daily, living joy.

Acknowledgement
My grateful thanks to Neil's brother, Clive McGovern for receiving me so quietly and polietly, when I arrived out the blue and out of the past, one fine summer's morning, and for accepting my story with such appreciation and enthusiasm.

CHAPTER 1

'What a crowd of vivid memories shared with you! What wastes of sand between these strung-out landmarks; not a sequence of lush meadows, but prevailing aridity and featurelessness, interspersed with spots of joy, flashes of wings and peacock hues,' wrote Neil, the apple-picker.

My story began, insignificantly, in the village of Deanston, which nestles in one of nature's little cul-de-sacs, beside the River Teith in Perthshire. Nothing ever disturbed the tranquillity of that idyllic hamlet unless it was the mighty river, leaping and swirling in its channels, or dipping and waltzing under the bridge near the Castle of Doune, as it raced on its way to the sea.

From my home in Falkirk, I entered this rural paradise with all the innocence of youth, early in my career, for as a young teacher, I wanted to extend my experience.

Nothing gave hint of the turmoil that would soon enough afflict me.

My only regret in leaving Falkirk was that I would see a little less of my friend Valerie, a teacher like myself. Valerie, was tall, attractive and talented; I was less attractive and had no talents beyond those for which I had been trained. Our friendship had begun when we found ourselves shipwrecked in the errant and impulsive seas of romance. When things went wrong for me, romantically, I was dead without Valerie, and in the times ahead I was going to need her more than either of us could have foreseen.

I soon established myself in a large and comfortable house and was the only teacher in the little school, along with the headmaster, the fat and jolly Mr Bain, for whom the happiest day in the week was Tuesday, when he would come into school, beaming and rubbing his hands in anticipation, eagerly announcing, 'Tuesday . . . doughballs to-day!' I had to thwart a cheeky desire to say, 'You do look as if you were in need of doughballs!'

When school was over, I walked through the meadows where cows grazed peacefully, listened to the buzz of filmy-winged creatures, climbed through the forests and felt the light rain on my face.

Nowhere was there a message of turmoil, though autumn evenings were violent enough, when shrieking gales raged through angry woods of silver birch and beech trees, carrying off in one great sweep, flurries of leaves, flashes of red and

1

gold. And even I seemed drawn into the movement of those October evenings, when the wind would tug at my billowing coat and toss me along in its path. How I loved it and how I laughed in those carefree days!

But might not the pessimist have been lurking in the shadows, and might he not at such a time have asked, 'What retributions are brewing obscurely for the reveller when everything is so arranged for pleasure?'

Though so much pleasure was clearly mine to enjoy, strange how I had to ponder some rare yearning within, as I sat in the summer shade of Castle Doune, idly tossing stones into the shallows of the river; a passion for something more, something deeper, more meaningful, that sought expression. Perhaps it was an inner rejection of these days of euphoria, that they were out of harmony with what I felt my life should be, for there was little outlet for giving, much more for taking.

Easter of '65 was approaching and I decided to take a walking holiday on the Island of Mull, a wilder place, where at least I would breathe Hebridean airs. I had hoped that Valerie would accompany me, for she had a boldness and audacity where boys were concerned, which acted as a foil for my shyness, and, though on occasions she could be constrained in company, the boldness she exhibited was more the impulse of the moment, an open, honest and uncalculating bravado, in which she became carried away. Unfortunately, however, she was otherwise engaged so I set off on my own for a few days.

That holiday was to make a great impression on me.

Seeking to reject sophisticated hotel life with its posh and comfort-seeking clientèle, I went for the simpler life of the hostel and the hospitality of the mountaineers and walkers.

On that pleasant day of my arrival on Mull, I made my solitary way across the island, enjoying the freshness, the sense of openness and freedom, until I arrived at the hostel on the seafront Main Street of Tobermory.

I entered the spacious common-room with its well-scrubbed tables, polished floors and kettles boiling noisily on the old-fashioned stove.

One young man sat alone in the big, empty room. It was his boyish youth that made him at once attractive. I laid down my pack and hung up my jacket and had just sat down at one of the tables when he approached and addressed me. I was slightly taken aback for shyness disadvantaged me, and with an air of slight anxiety he said, 'You know, the worst possible thing that can happen to a stranger has happened to me.'

I moved along the bench to make room for him and asked what had happened.

'A party of screaming schoolchildren has just descended on the place and I don't know if I can stand a lot of noisy kids.'

2

He looked a little uneasy and, sensing a bit of reserve on his part, I tried to be as friendly as possible.

'I'll tell you what,' I said rising, 'you sit here and I'll go and make a pot of tea and then we'll talk about it.' I moved off, trying to gather my wits and assemble some confidence. From the corner of my eye, I watched him, gathering impressions from his dress, bearing and posture.

'My lucky day!' I thought.

I returned with the tea and we talked for a bit and he must have felt more at ease, for he soon took out a pipe and lit it. I watched him. He held the pipe in his right hand, elbow on the table and blew a languorous curl of smoke into the air, adopting something of a pose, I thought.

'Well,' I said shortly, 'if we go for a walk we would get away from the school party.'

'Oh, I would love that!' he said enthusiastically. 'That's a great idea!' We lost no time in leaving.

It was a fine day as we soldiered our way across the winding roads of Mull, easy terrain too, neither rugged nor too demanding, just moorland, rising and falling gently, as the birds rise and fall in flight, and the grasses bend and blow in the wind, and the hills rise and fall away in a never ending rhythm of life.

He had come up from London and he told me his name was Alan.

'Well then, Alan,' I teased, 'there's nothing here to chill your fine English blood. No whipping wind, or cloud even, or prospect of a frenzied downpour.'

'That's right!' he said, as we marched along. (I had noticed his fine leather walking boots.)

'This is wonderful,' he enthused. 'I wouldn't have missed this for anything,' and I tried to keep up with his marching step.

I'd come prepared for a picnic, (I knew my genteel companion wouldn't have had a clue), and after some miles of brisk walking, I suggested a stop. When this was approved, I lit a fire in a mossy clearing on the edge of a piece of woodland, and he gathered twigs to keep it going while I unpacked a few sandwiches.

He sat with his back against an old stump of a tree and I sat opposite with the fire between us, with just enough life in it to produce wisps of wood-smoke that sweetened the air and gave that touch of intimacy to the atmosphere. 'Valerie, eat your heart out!' I thought.

'You know,' he said, after a few moments, 'I'm really so glad I came, and to think that I nearly didn't . . . and I would have missed all this.' It was a pleasure to see his contentment.

'You know,' he said, confiding, 'my parents didn't want me to come here, and they disapproved of my staying at a hostel,' and he smiled across at me.

3

'You see, when we go on holiday we always stay at the most fashionable hotels. As a matter of fact,' he continued, adjusting himself more comfortably, 'we *never* come to Scotland. My family has no desire to come here.'

'I see,' I said, not wishing to make a criticism or comment. Besides, I appreciated the confidence.

The tea had been brewing on the fire and I now poured him some. He had always wanted to see something of the Hebrides, he told me.

I found him interesting, and admired his honesty and gentle rebellion, and while he once more puffed his pipe into life, I sat there wondering about him. He had been in a confiding mood and the atmosphere between us was easy and friendly, and I genuinely liked him. I wanted to satisfy my curiosity about him, so after offering him another sandwich, I asked him what he hoped to do with his life.

'Well,' he said, giving himself a stretch and puffing more smoke into the air, 'my parents wanted me to make a career in politics, but I honestly didn't care for that, so I decided to study law.'

Brushing the crumbs from my lap, I ventured an opinion 'Well, Alan, I think you've made a wise decision, because my feeling is that there's no respect to be gained nowadays in politics. I mean, what credibility have politicians any more?' I said, warming to my subject. 'They've become so corrupt, that they can't be trusted. They're nothing but a bunch of opportunists who take us for a ride. Don't you think so?'

He sat back, looking thoughtful before he replied. 'I suppose I agree with you – up to a point, anyway – but can you blame them when the majority make it so easy for the minority to take them for a ride?'

Momentarily challenged by this hint of provocation, I replied, 'But don't you think that's a bit cynical, Alan? I would have difficulty, I think, in respecting *anyone* who could manipulate the system for his own ends.'

He leaned across and put a few more twigs on the still-sparking fire.

'Well, maybe not. One does want the respect of one's contemporaries, but, let's face it, if people are so naïve they probably get only what they deserve.'

'But if they can't see that the system is using them – that is to say, if the poor of the earth are dispossessed – you wouldn't feel it a priority to help them recover their inheritance?'

He sat composed and comfortable in that quiet and unsullied glade of woodland.

'No, I wouldn't feel it a duty. Perhaps I'm not so well disposed towards my fellow man as you, but then the poor have only themselves to blame for their own lack of inheritance.'

4

'That may well be true,' I persisted, 'but in such a corrupt and unequal world, surely you can't be indifferent to their fate?'

I was relieved to be holding my own in this conversation for he was clearly much better educated than I. Besides, I was leading him into the 'territory' of mind I was happy in, like a mischievous pied piper.

He flicked away a hovering moth of late afternoon.

'Well, I can only say that you seem to have a charity and kindness which I don't have. You might aspire to the heights of perfection but that's not for me. I want to be affluent and successful, but I would want to be decent with it. Don't you want to be affluent too?' he asked as he spread himself more comfortably on the mossy stones, composed and at peace with the moment.

'I suppose I do, Alan, but I wouldn't want to have so much worldliness that I would lose touch with all that makes life so worthwhile,' I said, recalling the luxurious life at Deanston, which had begun to pall.

Nothing disturbed the peace of that quiet, intimate interlude, only the peewits sweeping across the moor. But how different we were in our backgrounds: our roots had fed in different soils; we had neither breathed the same airs nor been refreshed by the same rains. Yet, there he sat, a nice companion, in no hurry to be away, tenderly responding, and where there might have been a frosty stare, a curling lip, or a silence that was sullen, there was only a refreshing exchange, a meeting of souls.

But the afternoon was wearing on and it was time to get back on the road. Kicking the earth over the last remnant of glowing ember I told him it was time to go and I gathered my things. Happily enough, he rose, shook his jacket and we set our noses once more towards Tobermory.

Just as we started our brisk walk, friendly intimacy gave way to mischief and in a burst of energy renewed, I called out, 'Let's sing a marching song!'

'And let's keep in step!' he laughed.

Well aware of his different background of class, and recalling the words of a marching song my socialist mamma used to sing, I shouted into the wind:

'Comrades the bugles are sounding!

Shoulder your arms for the fray!'

With equal verve, he called out, 'I cannot sing,' and to my surprise, he jumped on a tree stump, shouting, 'but I'll make a speech,' and he made a mock speech.

'Are you addressing parliament?'

'I am,' he replied.

'Then come down from your platform, you corrupt politician!' I shouted, pulling him down.

'Rule Britannia!' he shouted, and we laughed enjoying the nonsense. Then I

5

jumped on to the stump.

'Don't listen to him!' I called, startling the birds. 'He has no feeling for his fellow man! He supports privilege! He's a cynic.!There's no place for him in this land!'

And he pulled me down, as a flock of startled plovers soared into the air.

We continued on our way, laughing.

'You've been such good fun, Alan,' I said.

'And you've such a gift for friendship, you've made this a great day!' I pretended not to hear, but I heard.

I was sorry that he was going home the following day, for I felt such a growing fondness for him and I knew I would never see him again and the fun of that day would soon enough pass away into memory. It made me recall the words of Housman:

'Ah, that two and two are four,
And neither five nor three,
The heart of man has long been sore,
And long 'tis like to be.'

But I was soon to learn that the day was not yet over, for he invited me to have a drink with him in a local bar, an invitation I cheerfully accepted.

He helped himself to some fine malt whiskies, which got him rather merry and he began to hum a Scots folk song asking me if I knew the words of it. When I said that I knew it, could teach him the words of it, *and* could sing it, he was absolutely thrilled and insisted that we go out into the night so that I could teach him. And that's what we did.

Before that day had come to an end, there was one final, curious episode in the day's events, which would herald a strange new era into my life.

We entered the hostel late. The children had been long in bed and silence reigned. In the common-room the old range still burned welcomingly, and the place was deserted, except for the presence of one young man, who read. He did not look up. I felt a strange stillness in the room, an atmosphere I can't describe, which communicated an instinct in me to disturb nothing, open no conversation and, had I been on my own, I would have slipped off quietly into the night.

However, Alan, not at all perceptive of atmosphere in his semi-inebriated state, jumped rudely, you might have said, into the fragile porcelain stillness of the room, and shattered it.

'I say!' he burst out with enthusiasm, 'We've had the most wonderful walk to-day, this girl and I, and she's been the most marvellous company!' By that time of night, I was tired and I was embarrassed at more attention. The youth looked up and smiled, placing his book down on the table. He was a fresh, pink-faced youth with raven-black hair and a gaze of some concentration, and to hide my confusion, I offered to make some tea.

At the mention of tea, up jumped the youth in a flurry of goodwill and there was not a part of him that did not jerk with happy animation.

'Sit where you are,' he entreated, 'I'll make us all some!' His arms and legs fled with feather-like agility, and soon, with small convulsive leaps, he was back.

I was then further embarrassed when Alan recounted to the youth the exploits of the day, which were by now, perhaps, a little larger than life.

'By the way,' he said to the new chap, 'was it you who arrived late last night?'

'Yes, it was.'

'Then do all these objects scattered over the bed belong to you?'

'Yes.'

'You don't say!' said Alan, highly amused. 'Where do you find them. Do you collect them, or what?'

'I've been collecting things since I came on holiday. Mainly I find them on the shore.'

'But it's a load of old junk!' said Alan, highly amused and unable to conceal his surprise.

'There are bones, shells, stones, wood . . . you've even got an old hat!' he said good naturedly.

The youth was enjoying this as much as Alan was.

'But anything I find on the shore really excites me,' he said with growing pleasure, and the conversation bounced like a ball between them. 'I'm proud of them,' and he lifted the hat into the air for it was beside him. 'This hat especially thrills me,' he said. 'It may once have belonged to an old sea captain; it enlivens my imagination,' and in an agitation of excitement, went on to describe how and when he found it.

The conversation grew livelier. Words poured from the happy youth like quicksand, and his cheeks grew pink with pleasure.

'And are you taking them home?' I asked.

'Oh, yes,' he said, with an enthusiasm that surprised Alan.

'But won't your family mind?'

'Oh, yes,' was the emphatic reply. 'They'll object. I'm in for a reprimand anyway when I get home,' he added merrily.

'What about?' I queried.

'Oh, about the disgusting state of my hair and my clothing. My parents will say what a wreck I am and a disgrace to the family,' said he, warming to his subject and with a mischievous gleam in his eye. 'It always happens,' he said.

'And what will you say?' asked Alan.

'My reaction to that,' he said, clearly enjoying himself, 'will be to exaggerate my distaste for cleanliness and provide them with an imaginative selection of details from my week's experience,' he grinned.

'Well done!' I said. I found myself listening attentively.

'What's more,' he added, 'I've already had a letter from my mother reprimanding me.'

'What about?' I asked with growing curiosity.

'Well, simply because I had referred in an open postcard to the fact that I had not had a bath for a disgraceful period of time, and my mother was afraid that my insanitary habits would be blazoned abroad for all to hear and sniff at. You see, open postcards are read aloud in the village post office.'

'Well,' I joked, 'just send another postcard informing the family that you've had a bath every day in the local river and dried yourself in the heather, and that you're the cleanest hosteller in the Highlands!'

'A good idea!' he rejoined. 'I'll despatch another card, with the sublime information made public that I've had a bath every day, that I'm a paragon of purity and cleanliness, an honour to my profession, that I've not disgraced my noble lineage of Celtic chieftains and conclude with the pious hope that long life be granted to all makers and takers of baths, and all the village may now rejoice!' What tremulous vitality pulsated in that insubstantial frame.

I confess my eye was firmly fixed on this sprite, this child of fun. I found the playful riposte rivetting.

However, it was getting late. We sat more quietly for a bit before Alan asked if he was leaving the next day.

'Yes,' said the youth, whose name was Neil, and who came from Gloucestershire.

'I'm leaving too,' said Alan. 'I would have stayed longer but I have to be in the Courts on Monday morning. I'm beginning my training as a barrister. What do you do, Neil?' he asked.

'I'm hoping to get a job as an apple-picker when I get home,' he answered, his face wreathed in smiles.

In this good-natured atmosphere, Alan threw caution to the wind and spoke, I thought, a little insensitively.

'An apple-picker! What kind of profession is that for a bright chap like yourself?'

'Well,' said the youth undaunted, 'what's wrong with that? If I were a barrister say, like yourself, I feel that would probably debar me from becoming an apple-picker, or, for example, from becoming a dustman.'

'But surely you don't want to become a dustman?' replied Alan, outrageously.

'But yes, I would wish to have many insights into human nature and society.'
Alan addressed him more soberly now, and I found the performance beguiling.
'You think then, that we should do many different kinds of work?'

'If one did many different kinds of work, then that would give one an imaginative sympathy with, and an understanding of, others' lives; one could acknowledge the equal social worth of many different occupations, with an inner conviction,' he said with disarming sincerity.

I recognised the apple-picker's lightness and fleetness of mind and warmed to his clear thinking humanity.

Alan had to pause to gather his thoughts, but tiredness was overtaking all of us and Neil was the first to recognise it.

'Please don't sit up late on my account,' he said, and looking at Alan, continued, 'You look tired, Alan. I would ramble on all night telling whimsical stories or boring you with senile jokes, with as much to provoke laughter as a hard-boiled egg! Besides, you have an early start.'

Alan decided it was time to go and, excusing himself, went off to bed.

It was now very late and why I lingered I do not know, but I found myself telling Neil that I had arranged to warden a hostel during the summer holidays in a wilderness area near Ullapool, and was surprised to discover that he too was voluntarily wardening for a summer spell in an area south of mine, near Diabaig.

'Maybe I'll come and see you,' he said.

'I wish you would,' I replied.

I was looking forward to my stint, for I liked to be among people and generally I was well liked, probably because I had no extreme of personality; neither was I very clever nor very talented. In other words, I hadn't enough character to prove formidable to anyone: there was no challenge.

I was fairly surprised, on asking him how he would feel about it, to be told, 'I'm a bit nervous, actually. I'm afraid that I might become a bit formidable.'

'Surely not.'

'Well, in the ordinary circumstances of living, I don't feel this. I'm not at all heroic in any way, yet when I feel confident I lose a sense of place, and then I just become silly,' was his reply.

I felt that by then I'd said enough, and it was time to go to bed. After clearing up, I too excused myself and the following day we all split up, going our separate ways.

After all the companionship and healthy intercourse with different kinds of people, I returned to my quiet, solitary life once again, knowing that I'd recall, with nostalgia, every event of that day I had spent with Alan and every word spoken.

CHAPTER 2

I returned to my solitary life all right but wasted no time in rushing off to see Valerie for my emotions were in turmoil, and when my feelings ran wild, she was my repair kit, my emotional ambulance.

'Oh, Valerie! I've got to talk to you!' I burst out, as soon as she opened the door.

'I met this wonderful chap on Mull,' I exploded, and she stood aside to let me barge in. 'Oh, let me tell you about him, Val! I just can't believe that I'll never see him again!' I gasped as I hurried along the hall.

She ushered me into the lounge, slightly frowning. 'He was just a dream Val, up from London on holiday on Mull,' and I threw myself into the armchair, which she pulled towards me.

'And to think I'm never going to see him again!' I paused to catch my breath. 'Oh, tell me what I'm going to do Valerie!'

Now, hold on!' she said bluntly. 'Take your time and start at the beginning. Who is this guy you're never going to see again? You met him on Mull?' and she pulled a chair over beside me.

'He was so nice, Val – middle-class, Oxford background – oh you would have liked him!' Still somewhat ruffled by the intrusion, she took off her specs, laid them on the table beside us, and arranged herself comfortably. 'Now, take a deep breath and start at the beginning,' she instructed. I've all day to listen to you. You went to Mull and you met this super guy. So, what's the big deal?'

'Well, I met him at Tobermory. Alan was his name. He'd come for a holiday but his parents disapproved of his staying at a hostel and meeting folks like me, but he came in spite of them! What do you think of that, then? Wasn't that special?'

I waited for her reply.

'Sure. And you liked him. So what?'

'I'll tell you what,' I said impatiently. 'Imagine a nice chap like that coming into my life then going out of it again, that's what!'

'You didn't get his address?'

'Valerie, I'd only just met him! He left the next day. You can't go asking for an address after just one day!'

'Well, I'd sure as hell ask for an address after only one day! You blew your chances!'

'Oh, don't be so hard on me, Valerie.'

'Anyway, go on. Tell me a bit more, I'm listening,' she softened, showing a little more interest. 'Did you say he was handsome?' and placing a skinny elbow on the arm of the chair, she leaned forward, gazing more intently.

'Well,' I continued, grateful for her attention, 'I don't know what you would call handsome, Valerie, but for me he was handsome all right, in a finely built sort of way, a genteel breed of middle-class undergraduate – you know, the pipe smoking type – about to train as a barrister.'

'Was he good company?' Valerie was blunt maybe, but she would hear me out.

'Great! And guess what, Valerie? He said I was great company too! Makes you wonder what he's been used to!'

The more I spoke, the calmer I became, and how healing it was for me to have Val to talk to, and how grateful I was for her patience.

Feeling a bit more relaxed, I added, 'Oh, I wish you had been there Valerie, it was great to be alive!' said I, beginning to dream again. 'It was one of those rare afternoons, fleeting, but full of happiness. Don't you feel it's great to be alive sometimes? I suppose it was something to do with the freshness of spring and the winds and the life in the grass and in the trees. Oh, you must feel that sometimes, Valerie.'

'No, I don't!' she snapped crustily. 'To me life's more of a burden than anything else! Anyway,' she continued, 'one minute you're broken-hearted and the next, you're on about the raptures of spring!'

'Well,' I said, wistfully, 'I hope falling in love's more to do with the raptures of spring!'

'It wouldn't have worked out anyway,' she said, gloomily. 'He sounds a bit too upper middle-class for your taste. It's not your scene.'

'Oh,' I said laughing, 'I see you class me with the riff-raff!'

'Well, I don't exactly see you in London's West End, sipping afternoon tea in the Ritz with a barrister,' she said insultingly.

'I see. The Ritz in Rothesay, maybe, but not in London!'

'I think that's about right!'

She never took me too seriously, thank goodness. It was 'water off a duck's back!'

'Anyway, you're probably right. It might not have worked out but not because we didn't share the same values. I certainly don't care for the middle class – you know, the outward respectability, elegance in dress, manners and accent, public

11

schools, that sort of thing, everything that elegantly covers up the vulgar love of money, but it's more to do with the knowledge of being out of my depth intellectually.'

Valerie began to shuffle a bit with impatience. 'But for God's sake, you only knew him for a day!'

'Well, I'm going to miss him like hell! I take it hard, Val. I'm not like Thomas Hardy's Elfride, "She swallowed the whole agony at a draught!"'

'I mean,' she persisted, 'it couldn't have been all that romantic,' as she crossed one elegant leg over the other, her eyes betraying an inquisitive look. 'Was it?' she asked, fidgeting with her beads.

'Well,' I said, rejecting the gloomy influence she sometimes spread, 'it was romantic for me. We were having a drink in the bar, the night before we left, and in the course of the evening he asked me if I knew a folk-song, and he hummed it to me. When I said I knew it, he insisted on my singing it to him, so off we went out into the night. We wandered along the deserted shore of Tobermory Bay, the waves splashing at our feet and the lights of the village twinkling behind us. The moon and stars were out that night, and as I sang I seemed to hear my voice float away on the night air, over the bay to meet the haunting call of the gulls out on the far sea waves. Valerie, it was a romantic moment to savour, and he seemed transported because my voice was the only sound to disturb "the silence of the seas, beyond the farthest Hebrides," and that was as much romance as I could ever hope to have,' and I sighed with the memory of it.

'And that's it?'

'That's it.'

I felt that the recollection of that warm memory was all the repair my soul needed.

'I don't know what I'd do without you, Val. You're the best medicine I have.'

Soon afterwards I left and, though much calmed, the knowledge that I would never see him again was a painful one and that night, lonely and alone, I wished to feel a silence 'That I might lose my way. And myself.'

I didn't see Alan again, but I was to see 'the apple-picker'.

CHAPTER 3

After my romantic break at Easter I resumed my uneventful work at school, uneventful not in the sense of meaning a dismissal of the children, for they were sweet and happy pupils, but in the sense that there were few problems of any serious proportion such as I would find later when I went to teach in Glasgow.

Life in the big house, with all the space I had to live in, and all the time at my disposal, seemed to reflect back the loneliness of it all, and as the weeks passed and summer drew near, my mind began to wander to the Highlands, where I would soon be going to warden at Achiltibuie near Ullapool. I wondered what the weather had been like and whether the hostels had been busy or not, and then my mind drifted back to Mull, and only then did I recall that the 'apple-picker' would, at that very time, be ensconced in his hostel and could supply me with all the information I sought.

Being incorrigibly impulsive, I despatched a scribbled and undistinguished letter and it brought a near instant reply, a startling reply, a letter unlike any other I had ever received before.

In reply to my asking him what books he had been reading, among other things, whether Agatha Christie, Jeffrey Archer or Karl Marx, he told me he had an enormous anthology of Dr Johnson's writing and that he loved him both as man and writer. He lost no time in suggesting that I read Boswell's great *Life*, and continued, 'Allowing for different expectations and ideals in the eighteenth century and Boswell's passion for exhaustive documentation and detail, the biography is perhaps insufficiently lively for a modern taste until the second volume. But I think you will like it.'

'Quite a bookish chap!' I thought. 'Must assume I'm bookish too!'

He had taken his Bible, he told me, but it had lain largely neglected.

'I came here to tackle my metaphysical doubtings. I have solved nothing,' he wrote. 'Indeed, I fear I'm more of a pagan than when I first arrived.' He said he had taken his Bible in the first place because, shortly before he left home, he had attended a funeral and, as he explained: 'I was shocked by the unfeeling professional slickness of the mourners, and the undignified curtness and superficiality of the service. I took refuge in laughter and that shocked a lot of

13

people much more.'

I found myself smiling as I recalled the personality of the apple-picker I'd met on Mull with his firmly held opinions and his confident self-assertions, and his response seemed somehow in character.

I soon found myself smiling again when he wrote of reading Ecclesiastes.

'I count Ecclesiastes a friend,' he said. 'He is so irreversibly despondent and plunged in gloom. What a marvellous fellow to have at a party. "All is Vanity" he'd lugubriously intone, taking an enormous piece of cake. "What profit hath a man of all his labour under the sun?" he'd add, his chin dropping its lowest droop of melancholy, as he sipped his seventh glass of port. "There's no hope for any of us" he'd conclude, amidst gales of sympathetic laughter.'

In reading Ecclesiastes he was not being pious, he said, but he liked the gloom. 'The spirit of opposition within me is provoked by a intrusion of pessimism into tolerably good humour. Ecclesiastes' shortcomings are displayed clearly in an extended reading, – narrowness and monotonous repetition.'

His letter continued with quite beautiful descriptions of Rosshire and the area in which he was living, but I was beginning to feel a bit overwhelmed by the scattered literary references as well as the descriptive pieces, and I'd never read Dr Johnson, nor had I ever looked at Ecclesiastes.

'There's more to the "apple-picker" than meets the eye!' I thought. I was beginning to get the wind up!

He admitted that there had been a time when he had felt sad at Craig.

'I've been trying to solve the great mystery of human happiness,' he told me.

'Like Tolstoy, I'm not sure that I can believe in the possibility of human happiness. I take the tragic view with the ancient dramatics that social, political and scientific advances cannot touch the heart of the human situation.'

By this time I felt a growing consternation, for I remembered that I had invited him to Acheninver and I was neither bookish nor scholarly, my profession demanding no more than the dramatic adventures of 'The Three Billy Goats Gruff!'

By the time I had read the letter in its entirety, that is to say, by the time I had perused the total package – descriptive, literary and philosophical – alarm bells were ringing!

Worse was to come when I realised that I'd teased him about reading Karl Marx, with the idle pretension that I was reading it, which was a silly joke, not to be taken seriously. But now I was in trouble, for he promised to begin a study of Marxism in order to 'demolish' my arguments 'from a position of strength!'

By then, I'd almost freaked out!

His manner of ending the epistle contained a hint that he hoped for a reply.

After apologising for the gloom in parts of his letter, he prescribed himself thus: 'Lord of Craig, my other titles I here abjure, they're such a numerous breed, and so defamatory. Don't trouble to reply, unless I've provoked you past silence.'

There was so much crammed into the letter that I had to read it several times, each time with much enjoyment and although I felt in awe of his creative piece of writing, my overriding feeling was one of humble gratitude that my letter of frivolity and meagre substance should provoke such industry, originality and charm that I felt I was being paid the sweetest of compliments. And I, almost a total stranger.

But the fact of the matter was that this bookish and very interesting person was about to visit me at Acheninver and the thought of meeting him inspired awe. However, I did make use of the library to acquaint myself with Dr Johnson.

His letter had arrived as I was about to leave for Acheninver so I sent a brief acknowledgement, describing my aristocratic life at Deanston, the shameful self-indulgence and the desire to relinquish the 'sweet repose upon a featherbed of isolation'. I looked forward to his arrival, I told him untruthfully, for I was almost a nervous wreck at the thought.

Unfortunately, Valerie could not accompany me in the summer as she was going to the States to visit a boyfriend.

I set off for Acheninver in the village of Achiltibuie, north of Ullapool, where I would spend the summer, and my work there lived up to my greatest expectations of it. The hostel was a converted croft which had belonged for generations to the family of the local headmaster, and it was situated in an area of mountain, moorland and sea, one of nature's masterpieces. At the back of the croft the moor led up to the Coigach range of mountains and in front, a narrow footpath followed the course of the river down to the sea, and beyond stretched The Summer Isles. No eye ever settled on a finer scene, whether of the Isles cradled in the seas, or raw winds battering the moors or blizzards blowing over the mountains. It was forever gripping in its natural beauty.

I was responsible for the efficient running of the hostel, its cleanliness, the general comfort of everyone, collection of payment and the enforcement of the rules, few and reasonable.

During;the day, adventurous and friendly people arrived to climb or walk and in the evening we would gather round the big Raeburn, while pots boiled and kettles roared, and relate adventures or misadventures and sometimes go down to the beach for a midnight bathe.

But always at the back of my mind was the knowledge that any day my genius of the pen would arrive and put me in a cold sweat; and when he did arrive, he was accompanied by a walking companion, a male friend from home, and that relieved me of his full attention.

During the first few days I saw no more of him than I did of the other hostellers; they came and went each day, walking or climbing, and evening brought the return of all the tired people to wash, cook and eat – a great mix of personalities. Unobtrusively, I watched him with the eagle's eye. I often saw him in a group round the big dining-table.

'He'll soon dominate,' I thought. 'His arguments will hold sway; his personality will prevail.'

He never dominated the conversation, but he could have done. He need not have borne fools gladly, but he did. He used his skill to ease people into conversation, encouraging them to take part. The more I saw of him, of his social skills and behaviour, the more I doubted my ability to meet the challenge that his company was going to be.

Fortunately for me, there was a gift of distraction in the person of John, a big, handsome, solitary, unfriendly and unsociable chap who had arrived a few days earlier on a powerful Japanese motor-bike. I couldn't help taking an interest in him.

The men's dormitory was immediately above the common-room and soon after 'lights out' when I heard soft snores from the dorm above, I quietly gave a final tidy round the common-room, let the fire burn out and put out the lamps.

John, however, instead of going to bed, sat there, long after midnight, reading by lamplight, then he would clatter out into the night to fill the coal pail, in spite of my protestations. According to the rules I could not retire until everyone else was in bed, so I just had to follow John like a shadow. He said nothing to me and I said nothing to him, but always, just before going to bed, he would make himself a cup of coffee.

He followed this procedure for the first two nights of his stay, and I'll never know what his thoughts about me were, but on the third night, or, if you like, in the early hours of the morning, he asked me if I would like a cup of coffee, just as he was making his own. I agreed. The following night, I got a cup of coffee and a piece of toast, but few words passed between us. Still these were friendly overtures not to be disdained.

Our near-silent, somewhat pathetic friendship developed, however, for John actually took me for runs on his bike into really wild wildernesses, not that it was in any way romantic, for I remember him throwing stones at me, but remember too, on another occasion, when I lay on the shores of a remote loch-side, half asleep, and cold drops of rain began to fall, he laid his jacket gently over me.

Later, he showed me how to trap moths by candlelight, took me over the moors to point out the many insectivorous plants which he named for me, as well as naming the hillside beetles and moorland bugs. John's post-graduate thesis was on 'Snails'.

My relationship with John reminds me of the poem, 'The Lotus Eaters', where the poet talks of 'Flowers, wooed from out the bud'.

But, distraction or not, the inevitable moment had arrived when Neil's friend departed and I agreed to his suggestion that we go on a walk the following day. During his stay, I had kept my distance, partly because of a natural lack of confidence and partly because he was simply a threat, for I did not know what to expect of him, nor which philosophical topic he might engage me in; and then, what would I do? He was not going to be satisfied with the exchange of common pleasantries but would expect the cut and thrust of argument.

I lay tossing in bed that night, trying to have answers prepared in case he should ask my opinion on, say, the tragic human situation, or the dialectical materialism of Marx or perhaps discussion of the schizoid tendencies in the poems of Sylvia Plath. Anything was possible! It came as no surprise, therefore, that I found myself in a state of near distress and the outcome was in the hands of the gods!

But, as it happened, the gods were quite good to me on that occasion.

He suggested a fifteen mile walk, which was not beyond my capability, but fifteen miles of intellectual conversation would be a crushing and impossible burden, so I was greatly relieved when he suggested that he would join the path at the Ullapool end while I should start at the opposite end, that is, some three miles from the hostel, and we would meet halfway.

He had chosen a dangerous cliff walk, which can only be undertaken in fine weather and one is advised to carry a booklet of instructions, as the path sometimes disappears and there is a steep drop to the sea.

So adventure was about to be thrust upon me, and though I craved adventure, I could never have it, being one of earth's fainthearted.

Walking I loved for the deep sense of security of foot upon the solid ground of Earth, but this path posed a challenge, for it was only faintly discernible across much ruptured terrain of broken and indented coastline.

John was good to me that day, although he was piqued when I refused to go for an afternoon on the mountains with him, but he offered to take me on his bike the three miles of road and see me off safely on the path. Before I left him, he suggested we go for a swim, but I had to refuse. I don't know what opinion he had of Neil but his parting words to me were, 'What do you see in him anyway?'

17

'The same as I see in you, John.'

My instructions advised that I follow the marked posts on the first few miles of track, and as soon as my eye fixed on a post I stumbled towards it, clinging tenaciously until I could see the next one. I was frightened but carried on, tumbling over boulders, losing my balance on the tussocks of knotted grass, scratching myself on the coarse heather, and frightened I might fall into the sea or lose my way. I began to look like a moorland beetle scurrying from a predator. The only relief came my way when, occasionally releasing my grip, I would look up and gaze around me to find myself amazed by such a panorama of unspoilt wilderness, gnarled, roughly-hewn and primeval, and so proud to be part of it, even humbled to have a little niche in it for myself.

As I conquered my way ahead, my cowardice lessened and my proficiency increased, and the sun still shone on an azure sea.

But after three hours had elapsed and there was no sign of my companion and, when I could see slippery and treacherous gullies ahead, I decided to have a rest on a grassy patch, and seeing the gorgeous *cicindella campestris* roving in the sun, gave me hope that I too might survive!

I was about to have something to eat, if only to cheat time, when in the distance I discerned a goblin figure and, flailing arms like a windmill in motion, gave me the clue it was he.

'Thank God! I said aloud, 'at least I'm safe!'

I was relieved when he approached and greeted me, for the sun had begun to decline and shadows fell across the path, but I was astonished when, like a powerhouse, he flashed past me, not stopping for a breath. With elfin trot, he shot up a steep incline, not tired, not breathless, and disappeared over the top. I was left standing there bewildered. But I didn't want to be left behind so I went running after him, fleeing over bog and stone, trying to keep him in sight. His figure darted this way and that. My tired legs were like rubber, sliding and skidding, first in one direction and then in another.

I was not amused. 'What have we here, anyway?' I wondered. 'Some demi-god, nymph of the sea, Deity?'

I had no option but to follow like a puppy after its master. The flesh and muscle ahead moved with the precision of a fine tool, while I hoofed laboriously. He did occasionally turn to check that I was there, and sometimes he called out to me.

At last he came to a river where he stopped and waited for me before crossing the stepping stones and extending a helping hand.

But I was still in a state of shock. Curtly I thanked him but refused his hand. He was taken aback as if I'd stuck a red hot pin into him.

'You might fall in!' he exclaimed.

'I won't mind. The joy is in the difficulty,' I replied tersely.

When he suggested we should eat and rest, I was so relieved that the tension left me. Because he had felt slighted I was a bit sorry for him, so I explained that I preferred not to have help, that I liked a bit of a frolic with nature.

'I'm glad you explained, for I thought you were being an "independent Scot".'

We sat down beside the river and I took off my wellingtons.

'You've not come in wellingtons,' he exclaimed. 'Why, that's suicide!'

'No you're quite wrong. I'm foot-sure.'

'Well,' he said, satisfied with that, 'I'll follow your example and take my boots off.'

So we undertook the first priority and bathed our feet.

I was just opening my bag of sandwiches when he said, 'Don't open your parcel of food,' and fumbling in his rucksack he brought out a small parcel.

'I was shopping at Ullapool and I've bought some specially nice things for us to eat,' he said, sitting down beside me on one of the flat-topped stones. 'We'll share what I have.'

But he brought out another parcel, and his bright intense eyes softened for a moment. 'And I've bought you a present,' and he handed me the parcel, which I opened, not quite knowing what to say or how to say it; but I was very touched to know he was thinking about me.

When I opened it I found a length of Harris tweed, fine and soft to the touch, and I expressed my thanks before folding it away.

To hide my embarrassment I changed the subject. 'I'm thirsty.'

He fumbled in his pack for a cup.

'I don't want a cup!' I said derisively, and I splashed him with water, ran off down the stream, lay face down and drank. 'Come on!' I shouted.

He got up from the stone he was sitting on and came down the stream towards me. 'But I'll lose my dignity!' he joked.

'So what'

'If I lose my dignity, I might lose my identity!' he countered.

'Well, in that case,' I said, 'we'll lose our dignity together, and who's to know?'

We played around a bit before sitting down again by a small waterfall. I felt more relaxed now that we had eaten and rested, and we just sat there idly tossing stones into the small pool.

'You know,' he said, 'I would love to bring my little brother and sister here.'

'What a good idea, and so you should!' I said.

'But they've led a rather sheltered life . . .' and he paused waiting for my response.

'But,' I said, a little surprised. 'this is a paradise for children. They would love it here.'

He thought for a moment before saying, to my surprise, 'John is a bit coarse and his behaviour worries me a bit. I wouldn't want the children to pick up that behaviour.' I knew John was anti-social but I knew too he had a good heart somewhere, though I didn't say anything about that.

'But Neil,' I said, 'John's behaviour would be a small consideration compared with the fun and the benefits it would give them. What a place for children! Think of the scrambling over hills and rocks, and all the fun they'd have on the beach.'

Then I said after a pause, 'Does John make you angry?'

'No one makes me angry,' came the strange reply.

After a rest and some idle and disconnected talk, we decided to make our way back, but to my astonishment he began to wade out to sea, not wishing to return by the way I had come. He called over his shoulder. 'The coastline looks astonishingly beautiful.'

Strange that I followed and trusted him.

When I found myself sinking in deep water, I called out to him and he returned to me, took my hand and led me on. 'Why covet an experience so inherently dangerous?' I wondered. We continued paddling slowly, following the coastline and, finally coming out of the water, we began an ascent of the rocks leading upwards.

'Do you realise,' he said mysteriously, 'that no one has ever been here before?'

We found ourselves ascending a wet and slippery chasm in a cold that chilled. We chose our footholds carefully and pulled ourselves upwards, but Neil insisted on going first. He made me promise emphatically that if he slipped, I was not to help him. Strenuously we exerted ourselves, and when his ankle was at my eye level, his foot suddenly slipped. I grabbed his ankle.

'Leave me!' he commanded. 'If I slip, there is nothing you can do for me.'

Looking down into the sea below, I agreed. Thus we scrambled until late afternoon had passed.

Eventually, after more walking, I could see the path in sight.

'I thought I'd never see the path again,' I sighed.

'Were you afraid?' he asked, taking my hand and helping me over a heathery pit.

Willingly giving my hand this time, I said. 'Yes, I was.'

'But I would have helped you if you had been in any danger,' he told me. 'I just didn't want you to help me, for that way we would both have come to grief.'

'But I liked the danger.'

'So did I.'

We had almost reached the end of the path, the beginning of the road, when Neil said to me, 'You know, none of my friends would have scrambled along the cliffs with me. It would have been too tame for them compared with mountain climbing. I'm so glad you were willing to share this pleasure with me. You're a sport!';

I was chuffed with that!

A hostelling friend of mine, Adrian, was waiting at the end of the road to take us back in his car.

Suddenly inspired when I returned I said, 'I know what Neil! Since this is your last evening, what about my arranging a farewell meal for you in the privacy of my room?'

'What a good idea!' he said. 'Whom will we invite?'

'Just ourselves,' I said bravely.

'Wouldn't it be kinder to have one or two more?'

'Sure!' I said. 'You choose.'

'Well, the chap called David seems a bit lonely. What about asking him? And would you like to invite John?'

'Yes, I would,' I said. John too, was leaving the following day.

'And we must have Bob and Adrian,' I said, for they were friends of mine from previous hostelling times.

They all agreed to come, except David.

'I'll cook a nice tea,' said Bob.

'I'll bake the bread' said Neil.

'I'll supply the tablecloth - my sleeping bag,' said John.

'I'll bake a dumpling,' said I.

'And what will I do?' asked Adrian.

'You can supply the cloth to wrap the dumpling in - your vest will do fine!' I told him.

Late that night, in the privacy of my little room, we ate a sumptuous meal by lamplight, but conversation was in short supply because the dumpling took a heavy toll.

'I'm feeling drowsy,' said Adrian, the first to succumb. 'I'm off to bed. By the way,' he said, addressing me, 'when will I get my vest back?'

'That depends on the river.'

'What's that supposed to mean?'

'Well, I'll have to put it under a stone in the river and it will take a few thousand miles of river to pour over it before it will remove the stain.' A big smile spread over his face indicating that he would be the proud owner of such a distinguished garment.

I offered more dumpling, but Neil said he'd have indigestion if he ate any more.

Bob, Neil and John were all leaving the following day, Rannoch Moor being the spot most dreaded by all where they always got battered with wind and rain. Talking of the journey home, plus the heat in the small room and the lateness of the night, all contrived to make everyone drowsy, and each left one by one. Neil said he'd never be able to sleep. His scooter was undergoing repair at Ullapool, twenty-five miles away and he had to catch the first bus in the morning.

So, for me, it was the end of a perfect day.

I deliberately lay awake all night so as to give Neil a call in the morning. I slipped into the dorm at five a.m. but he was awake.

'Oh, you shouldn't have done this for me,' he whispered.

I prepared hot milk for him to drink, with lemon and honey, for I knew he liked that, and I cleaned his boots. It was now six o'clock.

'I'm coming to see you off,' I said, tiptoeing quietly around and putting a piece of dumpling into his bag.

'You mustn't' he said, speedily moving from place to place, packing. 'It will tire you.'

'If I insist you can't stop me,' I whispered, throwing on my coat.

'Well,' he compromised. 'you can come half way.'

We moved off at a brisk pace into the early morning air but when the cool air hit my lungs, I felt myself sniff.

'Have you a hanky, Neil?' I asked.

He went into one of the deep pockets of his jacket and pulled out a grey, crumpled rag, looked at it, withheld it for a moment, gave me an intense stare, then passed it to me, expecting me to recoil. I deliberately didn't recoil, took it, blew my nose, returned it and we both burst out laughing.

Not much was said between us, for I sensed he was tense with the long journey ahead on a scooter which, by all accounts, was sorely wounded, and as I marched along the three miles of road with him, a memory came back of another road I'd walked along, some months before, with a quite different young man, now almost gone from my memory. His going had been sad, and now Neil was going and I was fond of him too in an odd sort of way. I had a strange feeling of emptiness as I approached the bus terminal.

The bus was waiting. The driver took his luggage.

'I hope you arrive home safely. Send me a card and tell me.'

He was boarding the bus. 'No, I don't want to' he called over his shoulder and I was taken aback. He explained quickly that he had once promised to send someone a card and by the time he got round to doing it, the person had died.

I watched him take his seat and the bus moved off. I was losing another acquaintance for whom I had some feeling. It was the moment for me to be brave. I waved good-bye and he, with more energy, returned my wave.

I ruefully walked back along the empty, early-morning road, clutching now and then at the errant wayside grasses, and gazing southwards towards the mountains of Ullapool, where he was heading. 'It's going to be a long day,' I murmured to myself. 'Tomorrow will come, and I will have forgotten him.'

And later that same morning I watched another departure, as John plied backwards and forwards between his motor-bike on one side of the river, and the hostel on the other, packing his gear.

Tall, ruggedly built, strong and powerful, my eyes followed him secretly. I found excuses to go outside. He looked at no one and spoke to no one, unwilling to befriend, yet with a heart not entirely closed. His mother had died when he was a small boy and perhaps he was getting his own back at life, which hadn't loved him enough.

The moment came when his gear was packed and I wondered only if he would wave me good-bye, would he 'bend' that much for me? He mounted his bike, made adjustments and moved off, up the track. I stood and looked and waited. My eyes followed the moving figure. Away at the top of the track he turned round and saw me. He waved good-bye! I waved – and I never saw John again.

Given half a chance, I would have eloped with him!

CHAPTER 4

Mail arrived daily at the mail box – a hole in the bank of the river – and every afternoon I wandered up the track, pulled aside the moss and grass, and rummaged in the hole.

Five days after Neil left my hostel, my eager hand pulled out an envelope with the distinguishing precise black hand of Neil's, not a card but a letter, neither promised nor expected.

'Yours is the first hostel in which the warden baked me a dumpling, dubbined my boots and saw me safely to the bus. If I hear henceforth that every male visitor will receive such treatment, I shall no longer be able to consider your kindness to me as a special favour. I shall die of jealousy! I shall compose a dreadful curse of misogyny, embracing all feckless women, that is, all women with any independent spirit!'

I skipped down the path.

The remainder of the letter was a description of his journey home during which his bike had given him all sorts of predictable problems. The silencer ceased to work as he was approaching the centre of Fort William, and he arrived, he said, 'In a symphony of popping, spluttering and grating, so acute that heads were turning and policemen were stepping off the pavement to accost me! But I got through,' he said, 'by crafty gear changing.'

When he got home, he said, his parents greeted him with dismay and he was hurt with such an unsympathetic reception.

'Now I'm off to be an apple-picker in Kent.'

But the good times returned again because Alistair, another warden friend of mine of whom Valerie was very fond, had arrived. Many an afternoon we sat outside on the moor under the rowan tree, and while the river gurgled beside us he played the guitar and sang. I built a little fire, baked pancakes, spread them with honey, and served them to him, and others.

Many a night myself and many hostellers dragged our mattresses out on to the moor and slept under the stars, or we'd race down to the sandy beach at midnight and bathe in the sea.

Mere acquaintances were kind too, and I remember an instance when my parents had arrived unexpectedly and, at the time, I was on the top of Stac Polly.

A doctor and his young son, finding my parents there, came to tell me; they climbed to the top of the mountain and drove me back!

It had been a long, happy and eventful summer, but eventually the revels had to come to an end, and inevitably I had to return once more to my solitary life, which carried on in its quiet and unexceptionable way, in the village of Deanston near Doune.

Late summer passed into autumn; the cows grazed, the leaves rustled in the breeze and the wind carried the message of loneliness. The days shortened and the evenings darkened and Nature prepared for its long sleep. My social, meaningful life had gone; I had not the emotional resources to cope with the isolated seclusion, and my vitality began to wane.

And so I dreamed.

One evening in early winter I came across the piece of Harris tweed, my gift from Neil on our walk along the cliffs near Ullapool. In the lonely evening I decided to make something useful of it and, as I sewed, my memory strayed to Hebridean shores and evoked an atmosphere of trailing mists and surging seas, and I laid my sewing down, and dreamed my summer dreams again. Then I wrote to Neil and asked him if he remembered our walk that day, and he soon replied.

'I have only vivid memories of Acheninver.

'I remember the perilous ledge which ascended gradually its walls of rock, and took us higher above a narrow chasm, in which the deep, green sea was pounding; and how it slapped against the stone, not rhythmically, but with startling irregularity, as if imbued with purpose. I am glad we saw this place and also that we turned back.

'I remember the steep wall of dripping mosses we tried to climb; that magnificent smell of earth and moisture and luxurious greenness; and the texture, not slimy, but amorously unresisting to the touch, so that the stroking palm is tempted upwards, more yielding far than velvet, smoother than marble, and with an exquisite coolness.

'I can see that place now, and feel the random drops of water on my brow, shocking and breathtaking, beautiful! I think of mermaids with trailing green hair, horses' manes, weeping-willow branches, each with the same falling flow of graceful beauty, and a vibrant energy and movement in their form; and the sunlight and sky and clear air, through which the eye sees what is. It is a secret place too. Not many people can reach it, and perhaps they miss it, or ignore it when they do.'

One of the nice things about Neil was the sensitivity that enabled him to

25

transform something ordinary into a memorable experience, a charm I warmed to, and which revealed all the time, more of the person.

While I benefitted enormously from the correspondence, I wondered what on earth he ever got out of it, and I asked him why he continued to write to one who must be such a bore.

Undaunted, he returned, 'Would I open the letters of a bore so eagerly and read and re-read them? I actually interrupted my dinner yesterday to read your letter. Witness your ascendancy over my animal instincts, over all that most makes me a man!'

His humour amused me and so I would amuse him. He'd commented so often on his dishevelled appearance that I bought a piece of brightly coloured flannel and stitched him up a face cloth, despatching it at once.

It brought this response: 'The flannel, apart from the humorous mockery implicit in giving such a gift, in connection with your well-remembered innuendoes about the dishevelled state of my appearance, arrived when I was marooned in bed, sweating and shivering and full of pain, anger and self-pity, as well as experiencing an endurable martyrdom that made me the focus of the family's solicitude and kindliness. In short, I'd succumbed to Asian flu. And to think of having such an undeserved gift from you! And to think you've been working away on a means to purify my external self while I was prostrate and further filth-gathering – the delicious irony of it!'

His letters when they came were great fun. But my lifestyle was wrong. I needed friends for survival, not letters. Confinement was damaging. In winter I was buried. Too much of myself and my life was focused on Neil.

Fate took advantage and swooped into this vacuum. Into my unchequered life came his letters, full of opinions, news, fun, buffoonery and even tapes of poems, music and literary pieces, all sorts of stimulating things from a cultivated mind, demonstrating a life of light and joy that spread outwards, like ripples from a centre of energy. I was becoming obsessed. I had no choice.

This relationship was bound to fail. He had gifts I could not match. Nothing lasting could come of a liaison so unequal. I did not deceive myself, but you don't jump off the roundabout when you're having fun and screaming with delight: you cling to it with the tenacity of a terrier.

It was time to have a chat with Valerie!

One winter's Saturday afternoon found me in Glasgow on my way to Valerie's.

What a city! What an atmosphere! I loved its working-class identity, loved its old Victorian buildings, even its drizzle; but best of all its heart that beat fast and full!

I jostled excitedly with the hordes debauching from the subway, felt the vibrations of lorries trundling past, dissolved into the crowds at traffic lights, gazed into shop windows and lingered on the steps of the library, catching snippets of conversation. I could have shouted for joy amidst all the bustle. I bounded along the wide pavements to Valerie's, past the elegant Victorian buildings, the private gardens and on to the spacious apartments of her home.

'Great to see you, Val!' I said, as I was invited to go in.

Unlike some of my friends, she was tidy and, typically, no books were scattered about, nor items of clothing, nor last night's coffee cups and saucers. The room was decorated in restful shades of green with carpets and curtains in matching shades of gold, which gave a sense of warmth. It was a room I was happy to sit in. Liveliness came in the form of two cockatiels, who gave a rendering of ear-piercing whistles from their cage in a quiet corner of the room, acknowledging my presence. I sank into the old sofa. She had been writing a letter, which she quickly put away, and drew a chair over beside me. Before sitting down, however, she breezed across the room like gossamer in the wind and placed a cloth over the bird's cage. 'We'll get no peace if I don't,' she said.

Valerie was taller than I, and more elegant. With her waspish waist she could wear the kinds of clothes I could only dream about, and on this occasion she wore a flowing skirt that hung in rich folds, and a matching silk blouse. Her hair was short and tidy with small natural curls that toppled glossily over her brow. When a little anxious, she would twist these curls with her finger. She wore spectacles which did not altogether detract from her femininity for they enlarged the dark pupils of soft, violet eyes. However, she was never entirely at peace with herself, for she often fidgeted and a sadness would often cross her face like a shadow.

I noticed something of that air when I arrived, but she soon explained that her visit to the States had been a disappointment, that her American boyfriend had treated her less than well, and that she'd decided to have no more to do with him. Valerie was a survivor and didn't go completely to pieces when an affair was broken off, because she'd never expected much of it anyway.

Well, she lost no time in her down-to-earth way of getting straight to the point, like an arrow to its target.

'Well, come on,' she said lightheartedly. 'Tell me more about Neil. It's ages since you wrote to me.'

'Where will I start?'

'Well, what's he like?' she asked, looking intently and full of expectation.

Teasing her a bit I said, 'Well . . . he's like lots of people.'

'Come on,' she tossed her head impatiently, 'you'll have to do better than that!'

'Well, I met him in the summer, and I liked him.'

'Yes, I know about that,' she interrupted impatiently, 'but what else? I mean, you obviously like him, but what's the big attraction? Is he good-looking?'

Glad to be the centre of attention I tried to describe the physical person, but I found it difficult. 'Descriptions aren't always easy for me, Valerie,' I said, 'because you can't separate the person from the personality . . . but, as far as looks are concerned, he's built a little like Alan, the chap I met on Mull, about the same height, average that is, and the same quite slim build. His hair is soft, very black and undisciplined, and he's always pushing two locks back from his brow. He's not nearly so handsome as Alistair, but I wasn't attracted to his looks so much as his personality; there's a sense of mischief and liveliness that makes his eyes sparkle and his face glow, and there's never a dull moment when he's around.'

'So . . . well, go on,' she said, twisting her beads round her finger.

I took my time now, trying to pin down my feelings and explain. 'Well, for example, when I'm bored he makes me laugh, and if I argue he turns my arguments upside down. He will tease me and clown a lot, until I begin to think he doesn't take life seriously, and then he proves me wrong again; and just when I think I'm getting my bearings, the needle of the compass suddenly swings round again.'

'Sounds odd to me, but go on.'

'There's something about his personality that's so compelling. I begin to think I know him, then I scratch underneath the surface and I find another person. He's not like anyone I've ever met before. In fact that's exactly what I told him.'

'And what did he say?'

'He said it was true I'd scratched his epidermis and that I'd punctured his skin, but he wasn't going to let me peel the infinite layers of himself, to reveal a nothingness at the core. That's how he put it. And what's more,' I added, 'when I mentioned his chameleon-like personality, do you know what he said?'

'No.'

'He said "he likes to project a little gallery of superficial contrasting personalities, none of which is altogether real. Life is sufficiently complex to allow that," and I started to giggle at his impishness.'

Valerie blinked. 'I see what you mean. A smart ass with a pen!'

'Einstein!' And I continued, 'But I'm mesmerised with the show, Valerie, as if I were at the circus with one dazzling performance following another.'

'OK,' she said, having twisted her beads into knots and still keen to listen, 'you haven't told me where he comes from or what he does for a living. Is he a student or what?'

'I don't conduct inquisitions, Valerie, but I know he lives near Stroud in Gloucestershire and he's just gone to pick apples in Kent.'

'Pick apples?'

'Yes, pick apples.'

I now had her undivided attention. She moved from the chair into the big armchair, stretched herself out and crossed her arms behind her head. I was grateful to be given the time in which to express what I felt; to explain, enlarge, confess and confide.

'I really like him, Valerie, and when he writes to me I'm over the moon, but, on the other hand, he's too knowledgeable, too intellectual; he's too much of a challenge for me. It's like nibbling forbidden fruit.'

'That's nonsense.'

'Valerie, you know how embarrassed I am when I'm out of my depth. I feel awkward and I begin to *look* awkward, a terrible combination. I think this strange new territory is not for me. It's like making footprints in virgin snow, or like an astronomer gazing at a new star.'

She shrugged her shoulders.

'Well . . . I don't know . . . what does he think about you, then?'

'God knows what he sees in me! But he encourages me to write, else I never would. I'm not so bold! He ends a letter on a question, and what is that but an invitation to reply? Or else he ends his letter on a provocative note which induces a reply. He wants me to write, but God knows where it will all lead.'

'Well, wait and see where it leads,' she said. 'You've nothing to lose.'

'I've everything to lose.'

'Sounds as if you think he's stuff that dreams are made of.'

'Yes, but not *my* dreams.'

'I'm off to get some coffee,' she said. 'And jam tarts.'

I rose, stretched my legs and looked out into the wide and busy Glasgow street and knew I would fare much better when I came to live in the city. When I left that evening, I knew it had helped enormously to have had Valerie to talk to.

CHAPTER 5

But starved and stifled as I was, in my rural heaven, I devoured his letters when they came and they sustained me.

He was my companion on my walks, and fragments of what he'd written and poems he'd sent me I carried in my mind. I clung strenuously to the very human interest that had invaded my sequestered life.

Two friends, Tom and Barbara, whom I'd met in the summer invited me to spend Christmas with them at Acheninver. I thought this would be a propitious time to invite Neil north, for I was going to have to take the plunge sometime and I knew Neil would love the Highlands in winter.

However, he was being interviewed for a job now that the fruit picking season was over, and since there was so much uncertainty surrounding the interview, he told me that he felt he could not come. 'It's left an empty space inside me,' he said, 'but we must arrange a meeting in the spring.'

Spring inevitably came and we were destined to meet at Barnard Castle in Yorkshire, a venue chosen by Neil as it was halfway for each of us to go. He would be travelling on his scooter and he kindly made travel arrangements for me to go by train.

The thought of meeting him again was a sobering one, for if I was going to be with him for any length of time, then I was going to feel my inadequacy profoundly. At the last minute, I got cold feet, and I told him I couldn't make the train. He made another arrangement and I cancelled that. These were clumsy attempts to put him off, but there was no real plan behind them, only an effort at stalling. My indecisiveness and vacillation brought a swift response.

'You are rather like an aristocratic customer to a downtrodden fishmonger. Let her dutiful servant scurry once more to do her bidding, let him trot along to the station, tongue lolling out, flick through the railway guide, discover the time and joyfully transmit them. I shall not be surprised to hear tomorrow that you will be unable to come, because you're required to guard the school's boiler and coal supply! Let's hope you will emerge from your sooty bunker, where you're doubtless knitting woolly socks for prison officers, and vouchsafe me a few moments of conversation. Please let me know!'

Before leaving, I gave Valerie a last minute call from school.

'I'm a bag of nerves! What am I going to do?'

'Well, you'll have to go!' came the retort.

With my light pack on my back, I walked away when school was over, turning now and then to wave to a little group of my pupils who watched my departure.

I'd been so preoccupied with apprehension at meeting him that I hadn't given a thought to the actual week-end, rather in the manner of repressing a traumatic experience by ignoring it exists, but once ensconced in the hostel I thought, 'Well, if the worst comes to the worst, at least it'll soon be over.'

When a message was phoned through saying he was going to be late, I sighed with relief and felt more able to relax. Small groups of chaps shot glances at me from time to time, and I smiled to overhear the warden tell them that I was waiting for my 'boyfriend'. Then he arrived, as large as life, hair flying everywhere, nose swollen with redness and face dirty.

'I'm sorry I'm late,' he apologised. 'Is my face dirty?'

'No, not really,' I lied, but of course, I could have said, 'you look as if you've just emerged from some sooty bunker!' If I had been capable of that much wit, I would have been less fearful in his company!

He was so dishevelled after his long journey I was aware of heads turning in our direction, which did not embarrass me, because the moment I heard his voice again, it brought an air of magic and evoked happy memories that stirred deep inside me, as music does when you hear it played again, after a long time.

We cooked, ate our supper and talked, but since he had arrived late, our evening was short.

My first memory of that week-end was my confrontation with the scooter, our sole means of transport.

Barnard Castle was a very busy little market town and we were in the middle of the Market Square on a Saturday morning. I stood on the pavement while he made adjustments to the scooter. I'd never been on it before. Feeling tense and uncomfortable standing there, a phrase instinctively came to mind. 'Now gird your loins.'

Being a naturally shy person I hated to be stared at, and there were lots of people around staring.

'Can I get on now?' I asked, feeling a need to get it all over.

'No, I have to run with it to start it.'

'You mean I have to run after you?'

'No. I have to take it half a mile along the road,' said he, ingenuously.

'You want me to walk half a mile along the road?' My voice was growing fainter. I shrivelled under the gaze of passers-by.

'No. I have to take it half a mile along the road and run with it to start it.'

'Then what?'

'When you see me coming, you'll have to jump on while I'm passing you.' He moved off. I just stood there feeling a creeping paralysis and wishing I could anaesthetize my feelings.

Suddenly there was a whirring in the air and a mass of small explosions. 'It must be he,' I thought, as an animated scrap, sparking and spluttering, came round the corner with him running alongside! I wondered at his energy. His face grew red as he ran, and thus was disclosed the secret of his sometimes red and swollen nose! With scarf streaming in the wind, he leapt on, like a musketeer into the saddle.

I saw him come towards me. He was cool and calm now. I did as I was told, but how I managed to throw one leg over the seat and manoeuvre into position I'll never know.

I only wanted to be out of that town and never to see it again.

On the outskirts of the town it came to a halt and we had to get off. Out of his pocket he emptied stones, string, wood, buttons and all sorts of bits of things. He selected a stone here, a piece of string there, stuck things in and tied things up, until miraculously the machine started again.

Thus we rattled along, spluttered to a halt, patched up its wounds and took off again.

'It's a bit awkward without a mirror,' he called back to me.

'You mean you can't see what's behind?'

'Not unless I turn round.'

The next thing he called was, 'The brakes aren't working too well either!'

'What does that mean?'

'Well, if I have to jump off I'll try to slow down so that you can jump off too!'

'Well, how very generous,' I thought.

'Have you got a licence?'

'No!'

Thus we travelled for fifteen miles, I clinging to him tightly.

We finally reached our destination and parked the scooter. I was glad to see the back of it. 'I think it needs repairing,' said he, somewhat understating the case.

We walked out over the moors and he took off his warm scarf and wrapped it round my shoulders and took my hand. It was a fine day, fresh and clear. We walked for a while before we said much. I chose to tell him about Valerie and a little about Alistair and that they were planning to spend a few days on Raasay, off Skye, at Easter.

'They say the view of the Red Hills of Skye from Raasay is spectacular,' I told him. 'They wondered if you would like to come.'

He thought it was a brilliant idea because he was hoping to spend Easter in Scotland with me. We discussed how we would travel and where we would rendezvous and decided that he and I would travel together and meet up with Val and Alistair at a point on Raasay.

'Let's take a tent or sleep in the open,' he suggested, but I warned against taking risks with the weather, for at Easter the weather can be treacherous.

'We'll take a tent then,' he agreed.

'And by the way,' I added, 'you'll have to keep me warm in the tent or I'll never sleep.'

'And you'll have to keep me warm too,' he responded. 'I couldn't bear to lie awake while you slept, listening to the rain beating on the canvas, and to your rhythmic and complacent breathing. I should be compelled to wake you.'

'Oh, you would! Then you'd better have a good excuse for waking me in the middle of the night!'

'Oh yes, I'd probably say, "Remind me to buy black pepper the next time we're in the supermarket!"'

As the weather was so fine, we slowed down our pace.

We talked of his family, for he occasionally mentioned them and I knew he was fond of his little brother and sister since he sometimes described the games he played with them, especially on the beaches in summertime when the family took a holiday.

He mentioned his father more than he spoke of anyone else in the family, and when he did so, there always sounded, for me, a note of discord. He seemed a complex person, not easy to define, who did not enjoy good health and was often tired and irritable. Homely family conversations often became angry disputations, 'absurd and speculative,' Neil told me.

'If my father and I discuss anything,' he said, 'he takes the opposite view which, as often as not, leads us into absurdities, but he's a man of high principle. You would like him.'

'Parents of "high principles",' I opined with some feeling, 'are often harsh and unyielding with children.'

We'd reached High Force.

'Oh Eilidh,' he said, searching out his camera. 'I must have a photograph of you.'

He asked me to stand beside the waterfall. I scrambled across, stuck my head in the air and gave a huge smile. 'Will that do?'

He wanted another shot and scrambled too close to the waterfall for a more spectacular picture. I called out to him, and then his foot slipped.

'You'll fall in!'

'If I were to fall in,' he returned, 'I'd sink to the bottom like a stone.'

'No you wouldn't. Your instincts would save you!'

'They would have no effect whatsoever,' he said emphatically.

Anything I ever said or wrote was the plain stuff of everyday without embellishment, decoration or originality and I found myself asking him if he was never bored with my letters.

'You've asked me that before,' he said, turning towards me and pausing. 'I keep all your letters to me. They mean more to me than all my books. You know that books can be bought, borrowed or stolen, but letters are unique.'

He was too generous to me, but my heart expanded. It wouldn't be hard to fall in love with him, and not because of his background, looks, class or education but because of something he said the first time I had met him, when he had spoken of the value of honest labour, giving it a dignity it deserved, quite an outspoken statement to have made, and one not often acknowledged.

We stopped now and then to look more carefully at the environment, while I pointed out a grass here and a wild flower there. He showed his curiosity by occasionally lifting a stone, stroking it, turning it over and, even on one occasion, licking it. I suppose for someone of imagination a stone must be an object of enchantment if one considers the history locked within it and the tales it might have to tell.

We came to a grassy clearing and we sat down to drink and rest.

'Do you know one of the reasons I like writing to you?' he asked.

I replied, with my confidence growing nicely, 'No, but I would dearly like to know.'

'Well, because you are so honest, I can tell you anything.'

'Is there something you want to tell me, Neil?' I said, sensing something.

'Should I tell the truth?'

'But you must always tell the truth, don't you think?'

'But what is the truth? Don't you think it might be distorted?'

I sensed the dread of intellectual conversation beyond my ability to respond. 'Well,' I laboured, 'yes, I've always felt there is no truth until you have transferred what you think and feel into words.'

'But,' he insisted, 'transferring what one feels into the medium of language may be distorted by prejudiced observation, jest, momentary whim, exaggeration.'

The only response I was capable of was, 'But you can only keep the principle of trying your best.' This was said without much confidence.

'But if one is inconsistent and unstable, so, too, is truth, shifting like sand before the wind.'

Perhaps I began to look tortured, for after a moment's pause he said, 'Hell's bells, I'm a tedious old poser, and you must be starving.'

I breathed more freely. 'Well, I suppose I'll have to accept your many shortcomings,' I said.

'Yes,' he replied, 'and all my ignoble characteristics as they choose to reveal themselves, in due course, and in intimate detail.'

'Then I'd better take to field and forest!' said I.

'How irresponsible!'

His deft fingers quickly opened the small picnic box, and as he did so I recalled his telling me that he'd embarked on an economy drive.

'I should have contributed something, Neil.'

'Not at all,' he said. 'Oh, I see you're referring to my austerity regime. Well, actually, I've been successful so I thought for your picnic we'd luxuriate in grapes, figs, bread, dates and a selection of cheeses.'

'All my favourites, and I shall tuck in with immodest greed.'

With these spread out before us, we tucked in.

I soon could see him kindle into life again and could see the mischievous glow in his eye.

'By the way,' he smiled, 'I meant to tell you earlier that I liked your arms enfolding me when we were on the scooter.'

'I was only trying to keep myself warm,' I replied.

'Well,' he laughed, 'as a radiator I can recommend you to all comers. But tell me,' he joked, 'am I no more than a radiator, no more than a rabbit?'

'When I am cold, Neil, I wish no more than the rabbit!'

'Oh, Disillusion!' he joked.

Then we talked of unconnected things. He apologised for not getting to Acheninver and he wanted to hear about my brief stay there.

I had a stupendous time and I told him how there had been a fall of snow the night before we left. Neil was packing away the picnic things.

'The whole area was transformed into a fairyland. It was the most beautiful sight I had ever seen, but Tom had to drive very carefully from Acheninver to Ullapool. The entire holiday was so perfectly arranged and managed, you would have loved it, Neil.'

His task of packing completed, he said nothing, but sat thoughtfully for a moment. I went over and sat beside him.

'Anyway, Neil,' I said, 'the journey would exhaust you. We'll arrange it again next year and you might manage.'

We sat for some moments before he said, 'I've always preferred the unknown to something that's planned. I hate following a plan; it precludes the unexpected.'

I was taken slightly by surprise because it was so opposed to what I felt, yet it made sense when I recalled our walk at Ullapool. And then he spoke in a quiet melancholy tone.

'My heart sinks when everything is arranged for pleasure. I see the fox congratulating himself, having just eaten a kid, and then he's immediately shot through the stomach with an arrow. Do you remember Hernyson's fable?'

'Vaguely . . . yes.'

'Then think of Greek tragedy and the inexorable fate of humans guilty of hubris, or Agamemnon conquering at Troy. What fate lies in store for them?'

'But that's too pessimistic Neil,' I exclaimed. 'It's wrong to think like that! You take too dark a view of things, and you think too much about death,' I said with feeling, for it was a criticism I had of him.

'But look around you, Eilidh,' he persisted, 'even here you see maggots multiplying in the belly of a dead deer, sheep's skulls bleached in the sun, bracken and fern struggling for supremacy in an acre of ground. One must be insensitive not to think of death, confronted with so many reminders of one's pathetic brief mortality.'

'But I don't take that view of life, Neil. It's just a rejection of all I've ever felt about life. It's not the whole truth.'

'Don't you think,' he continued, 'if plants and trees were capable of utterance and we of hearing them, would we not be deafened by their lamentations? I'm only saying what others have said, Eilidh.'

'You sometimes have that angle on nature, Neil. I remember you once described the call of the seagull as "hovering on the brink of expression but not to be appropriated by me," and that tells me the same thing about your dark outlook. I hate the thought of death too, and I must recognise it. I've always felt a great bonding with Nature, Nature which has nourished and sustained me and provided me with all the beauty and mystery I have even known; and why should I resent it that one day it will take me back? You've often told me, Neil, that you're not an optimist, that you take the tragic view with the ancients that scientific, social and political advances cannot touch the heart of the human situation, but my own experiences in life, my home and upbringing, have not led me to believe that.'

'Oh Eilidh,' he said, disconsolately, taking my cheeks in his hands in a movement of anxiety, 'I'm so sorry if I've made you feel unhappy. I didn't mean to. I know I am like this sometimes, but it's not the whole truth. You know that, don't you?' I nodded and he put his head against mine. 'You know I can be hopelessly frivolous and perverse,' he said, 'but don't despair.'

'I won't.'

But we'd been talking for long enough; afternoon was passing, clouds were racing and I was well satisfied with the success of the day, and we turned to retrace our steps.

We were passing through a clearing in the woods, when a streak of sun broke through the cloud.

'Let's not go back yet,' he implored, finding a grassy stretch in the clearing and holding out a hand for me to join him.

'You like to forget about time, Neil, when you're happy,' I said, lying down in the grass. He lay beside me, pillowing his head on my breast. I remember the raven black hair against the white of my blouse. I began stroking his hair.

I felt his hand caress my leg. He turned over.

'What are you thinking about, Neil?' I asked.

'Oh, I was thinking about Raasay in Spring,' he said, idly as he could.

'Did you say you were lusting after Raasay?'

'Oh yes! It's the Torridonian sandstone I'm lusting after!'

His hands stroked upwards.

When I turned towards him he could see that I was shyly embarrassed and reacted with exuberant nonsense.

'Oh, that's an odd sound your knee is making!'

'It's creaking with old age!' I laughed.

'Your doctor has just come in time. Let me get my hammer and test your reflexes! Oh! I don't like the look of this at all!'

'But, doctor, it's an artificial leg!'

'Ah, it needs oiling! That's annoying and disillusioning! I had such lecherous desires on your virginity!'

'Stopped you in time, then!'

'What a pity!'

After a few moments of this nonsense I told him he should write a farce.

'I suppose I could try.'

'What would you call it, then?'

'Obviously, "The Creaking Knee Joint" or "Virtue Triumphant", to be shown at the "Dirty Damsel Playhouse, WC1."'

I laughed, but the moments seemed suddenly long, for I couldn't keep this up. But he wasn't finished with his nonsense.

'Give me your hand,' he demanded. I offered my hand, not knowing what to expect of him. 'But a hand is so limited, fingers and palms only. I need a broader canvas when it comes to caressing - for a more flamboyant, sweeping brushstroke!'

'Well, a hand is all you're going to get, so see what you can do with it!'

'But my fingers are so blunt and coarsened, they need to be charged anew with life!'

'And what will recharge them?'

'Oh, they need contact with the ridges and depressions of deep and shallow flesh to be charged with life and feeling, but I must be content with a hand and see what I can do with it!'

'You've too much imagination, Neil.'

'Well, you've declined so gracefully.'

Then we kissed in such an unpremeditated way as if our natural selves were suspended and our instinctive selves were free.

'Ugh! Your chin is all bristly!' I exclaimed.

'Well, I wanted to snatch the forbidden fruit!'

'Did you not shave?'

'I thought I did. Anyway, you didn't manage to forestall the rape!'

'You're incorrigible, Neil!'

'Oh,' he gushed, 'but tell me you want all of me . . . spirit, flesh, lust. Everything!'

I laughed and said I'd had a wonderful day, but it was beginning to get cold and the afternoon had long waned. When we got back to the scooter, he wrapped his warm clothing round me and shyly kissed me. On the scooter I snuggled into his back. That night, before I fell into a deep sleep, I turned over in my mind the happy and interesting events of the day.

The following day saw us in a different area, not thickly wooded, but sufficiently so for him to lead the way through some gnarled vegetation, tenderly keeping little saplings from springing back at me.

He was happy just to wander idly and to be alone together, he told me and I was happy because I had enough to fill my dreams for many nights to come. It was like hearing a great orchestra playing in harmony, but the jubilant sound was not to last: there soon came the note of discord.

He had his arm around my waist and we came to a fence. He stopped there, took both my hands in his and drew me closer. I sensed he had something he wanted to tell me.

'You know, Eilidh,' he said quietly, 'I'm not a very happy person.'

Feeling my nerves tingle, I sat down and pulled him down beside me. Facing him I said, 'Is there something you want to tell me, Neil?'

How could he not be happy, the creator of fun and nonsense? I was taken by surprise, too, by the forlorn tone of his voice.

Whispering he intoned, 'Something went wrong in my childhood, Eilidh.'

All animation seemed suspended.

'My mother wasn't young when she had me. I was a delicate and sensitive child, my mother's first, and she pampered me a bit. I remember I cried once when someone called me "a pansy", and I seem to recall that my childhood didn't go well.' We relapsed into silence.

I didn't know what to say, but I had noticed that he spoke of his father quite out of context sometimes, and he mentioned him again, now. In hushed tones he said, 'My father and I are alike in many ways. He is a complex being like me and it has taken me a long time to get to know him.'

He continued with his sketch. 'Sometimes, asserting the existence of God, he'll point to the beauty of the view from the window and demand from where else this beauty derived if not from God. At other times, he'll boldly and bluffly maintain impossibly sceptical positions, but changing his ground with such bewildering swiftness that rational objections melt away. Priests, politicians, royalty, landowners and fellow workers, no one is spared from his uncompromising assaults once he's got the bit between his teeth. But he's become deeply embittered through enfeebling physical health, mental anxiety, insomnia and disillusionment with political parties.'

I let him talk on, then bravely I said, 'I don't think I would like your father, Neil.' However, I had no reason to believe that his father did not also have traits that were admirable.

'I don't think you're fair to him,' was all Neil said.

I let him say what he had to say, but I felt as if the sun had suddenly gone down and left an oppressive silence over the moors, except for the lonely call of the curlew.

'Have I made you unhappy?' he asked tenderly.

'No, Neil, it's just the silence of the moors; I find a bleakness on the English moors which I do not feel at home. I think we should go now.'

We walked back much more slowly and silently.

'I love the sense of peace here,' he said. 'I keep yearning for the wild places. I've been so tired and tense lately and had so many late nights that I've fallen behind in my correspondence. I've been writing letters for jobs – teaching jobs mainly – and I've had a number of interviews, and besides that, I've been reading a lot.'

'Is teaching what you want to do, Neil?'

'I don't know if a nine-to-five job really appeals to me,' he said. 'I often have stirrings, notions and temptations towards wandering, observing, studying, writing and not really towards regular work. But I'm determined to support myself, at least, and pay my own way, but,' he affirmed, 'you may assume I'm egotistic, cowardly, lazy and self-indulgent and will never contribute to society to the limit of my talent.'

'Maybe I could succeed in making teaching my career. Perhaps I could try it as a gesture towards conventionality, but maybe I hope to fail and so have an excuse to go the way I feel I have to go, no longer from selfish choosing but impersonal necessity.'

He continued. 'But you must forgive me for not replying to your most recent letter; it's just my habitual epistolary indolence which increases with time, like warts, fortunes and Prime Ministerial idiocy!'

'I don't expect you to answer my letters, Neil. You take things too seriously and you try to be perfect. You're trying to live at some austere height.'

'It's true humans need to slip and backslide and dodge and twist and postpone and borrow and muddle and idle; we cannot live at too high a level. The air is overpure and rarefied; we're fearfully exposed; the wind is piercingly keen, the view is unendurably distinct, we part for the smoky corruption, the familiar, comforting enclosure of the obscure and undemanding valley.'

'Yes, you live at some height which is too exposed.'

'I think,' he said, 'we are at home in neither hill nor hollow; we seek or are driven towards first the one, then the other, but are vagrants through this land, who settle nowhere finally.'

'But you have a lot of fine character, Neil,' I said.

'You're much too kind. But I feel a curious strength sometimes. It's often something like an imperviousness to ordinary pains and an inner certainty of later fulfilment and creative achievement.'

So there was another dimension to my gentle friend. This was not the witty and fun loving companion I knew, so full of the joy of living. There was something far deeper that blocked the flow of life and now, this morose and melancholy strain in his nature brought a confusion that constrained and tantalized me.

I felt like the fox in the fable, shot through the stomach, just when he had been congratulating himself in the sun.

We soon found ourselves retracing our steps, and after his telling me he wasn't a very happy person, we were walking much more slowly. Just before we reached the area where he'd left the scooter, he held his brow, saying he'd taken a headache.

I sat him down and hurried to a nearby stream and dipped my handkerchief into the water, and returned to place a cold compress on his brow. He closed his eyes. Several times I did this.

'Rest awhile,' I said.

'You've been so good to me,' he said. 'I take a headache like this about twice a year. Sometimes I get a feeling that my father is ill and when I go home, I discover that he *has* been ill.'

'Has that happened often?'

'No.'

'Well, that was just a coincidence.'

We sat for a while saying nothing. I stroked his head. It was all I knew to do to comfort him. I sat beside him, my body touching his. I sat looking at him, waiting for his colour to return, for he was pale.

'Do you know what I would do,' he said, 'if I were free of ties and responsibilities?'

'Tell me, Neil.'

There was a long pause. He put an arm round me, and drew me to him, and again, I felt drawn in to a strange new territory of sadness.

'I'd pack my bag, and take my notebook and pencil. I would no longer organise my own destiny, but wander as the wind took me. I should then be led, if there is any purpose in the universe, touching the humblest agent, to where I am needed, to "my place".'

His next words were to haunt me for a long time to come. 'Eilidh,' he whispered, 'you've been drawn to one born under an unlucky star.'

My very warm and human feeling felt a chill, as if a great sad breath had blown across the land.

Then the saddest of all came like the forlorn cry of one who has lost his way.

'You see, it's not just a journalistic turn of phrase to claim that I'm a prisoner of my own intelligence. This it was that made me an automatic candidate for Cambridge. I never wanted to go. I was entered for the scholarship examination, which lasted a week at Queens. I won a place. I had to go. I had to listen to fervent congratulations from masters, family and friends. I had to pretend to share the pleasurable anticipation of others. Then I had to feign enjoyment of college life.'

I listened to this like a child listening in awe to a fairy tale, in which all manner of strange, impossible and unbelievable things happen.

'After my first unhappy year,' he continued, 'I had a nervous breakdown, but I returned afterwards and completed my honours course. I was one of the top three students in my year. Having experienced the breakdown, I was left acutely aware of my own inner fragility. It is true that I have experienced rare moments of joy, but I often wish I could be free, pack my bag, and wander off.'

He stroked my head gently. 'What a catalogue of gloom I burden you with.'

The face of my world was taking on a different composition. Then he rose, saying, 'If we don't hurry, we'll have the moon for a companion.'

41

He got me to the station and gave me a quick kiss. I waved goodbye. He had a long journey home. I knew much more about him than I ever did before.

When I returned home, I was laden with mysteries of one who was so full of life you might have said of him, 'There is a madness about thee, and joy divine.'

But the next moment, he would be describing happiness as a state one could not hope to achieve. A sorrowful adagio would follow the exuberant overture. I was perplexed with the whimsical clown, turned mysterious enigma.

Maybe I had been drawn to one born under 'an unlucky star', but the sad revelations of that short week-end drew me even closer by the bonds of compassion, that most noble and compelling of emotions.

CHAPTER 6

Although life was still lonely, there was the bewitching time when I secured the little package from the postman. Waiting was the punishing time. After school each evening I went walking and each evening I returned, climbed the grey stone steps and entered the house. I hung up my coat. Nothing stirred. The house echoed the silence and the silence echoed the emptiness. I sat and I wrote. Next day, I eagerly awaited the postman.

And, oh, the cruel postman! the long wait! the ebb and flow of hopes! In the chill of the early morning air, I quietly opened the window and gazed along the street.

Patiently I watched, waited and listened. And then the dark form appeared. I closed the window, tiptoed to the door and waited motionless, hearing only the beating of my heart and feeling the tremble of my hand. Then I heard his step on the stairs, the shuffle outside the door. Was the letter for me - my neighbour? Then, when the steps receded, I tried to be very brave. It was the hardest thing.

Our epistolary friendship flourished. There were no secrets between us any more.

'The buds of love are beginning to grow,' he wrote, tempestuously. 'Draw me out of myself and see if you can love me!'

There was so much to love in him, but little of substance to me.

'It's too unequal,' I told Valerie.

In her blunt way, she responded, 'Oh, stop moaning!' We were planning to meet shortly on Raasay.

Letters shot like arrows between us.

Spring came. He travelled up to Scotland on his scooter to collect me on our way to Raasay, where we were to meet up with Valerie and Alistair.

So much had been said, it was the beginning of real hope and happiness.

The sun shone, the scooter sped, and light winds blew as we raced along the winding roads, through glens and by rivers and loch. We couldn't wait for fun and joy! I pulled his hair, nipped him, held him tightly and squeezed him. We stopped and tickled and cuddled and raced on. There was no holding us back.

'I think we are in for a great time!' I called to him, above the sound of the wind, for we were on the high road through Glenogle, near Killin.

At last we stopped by the roadside for a rest and parked the scooter.

'Even the scooter has gone well,' I said.

'Yes, like a Soviet rocket!'

'But Soviet rockets don't get a push-off first!'

'Maybe,' he said, 'but a forty mile embrace is not to be had for the asking every day.'

'I didn't ask!' and he took my hand and pulled me down the hillside.

'Let's find a private place, Neil.'

And, before long, we had a little grassy area hidden by a big rock that had tumbled from the craggs above. With my feet I flattened down some of the big tussocks of grass.

'Lie here beside me,' I said, pulling him down. 'Get a rest, Neil, for you've had a long drive.'

I lay back in the sun, head resting on my arms, totally relaxed.

'Ah . . . this magic. Can you hear the birds, Neil?'

'Yes, what a lovely spot this is,' he sighed his agreement, and lay down beside me.

Recapping on our previous letters, I said, 'I'm interested to hear that you've got a teaching job,' turning on my side to face him.

'And now that I'm teaching,' he said happily, 'I'll have a bit more money to spend.'

This gave me an opportunity to broach a subject that had been on my mind for some time. Pushing back the hair that fell over his brow I said, 'You have girls and boys in your class, Neil, and I've often wondered about the girls. You don't write to anyone else, do you?' I desperately needed reassurance, being me. I knew he would tell me the truth exactly as it was, that's why I felt some anxiety. I knew he prepared the students for Cambridge and I knew they must be so much cleverer than I, amongst other things.

'Yes,' he replied, 'some are clever, talented, rich, beautiful and well-groomed, but I've no difficulty in remaining impersonal towards any of them. Sometimes I think they are more bourgeois and blasé than ever. Fear none for a single second. I only refer to them in order to dismiss them.'

The words fell in blissful showers around my head. It was a record I would have played over and over again. I moved a little closer to him.

'Now,' he said, lying on his back, 'you've told me about Valerie. What about Alistair?'

'Actually, Neil, he stayed for a few nights at the hostel when you were there last summer; tall, blond, a gorgeous ensemble of health and happiness.'

'I think I recall him, but I didn't pay much attention.'

'I like him. He's good fun to be with. His was the first hostel I'd ever stayed at, and he was kind to both me and my parents. I will always be grateful to him for that. Although he's a minister, I don't think he takes his theology too seriously, at least I've never heard of his losing sleep over principles of church dogma! That's the problem with the Church. One looks for a direct answer, but it is evaded, but I think it's just in the nature of religion to be that way.'

'I know what you mean. There was a bishop on the television the other night who was asked a question about the Church's position on birth control. He evaded an answer in every possible way, pseudo-technical vocabulary, long-winded historical preamble and back-peddling, shuffling evasions, and then concluded with a hope of peace between men, broad smiles, hands piously clasped over the displayed Bible, breast cross flashing in the studio lights, chins resting comfortably on one another, the fat, well-fed face relaxed into an expression of benignity, producing an absolute pudding of empty benevolence!'

I laughed and he pulled off his warmer garments.

'I can't believe this heat at Easter!' I said, throwing off a jumper, and kicking it aside.

He came closer and his arms began to caress me.

'Do you remember what you said about throwing off uncertainties and inhibitions?' he asked provocatively.

'Did I? That must have been in one of my wildly impulsive moments!'

'And you asked at what temperature my passions burned?'

'I must have been a fool!'

'It's a dangerous question.'

'Now, Neil, remember *The Tempest*:

> "Give not to dalliance
> Too much to rein
> The strongest oaths
> Are straws to the fire in the blood!"'

I lay back on the grass.

He sat looking down at me, pulling back the idle strands of my long hair.

'I see that your fingertips are beginning to explore,' I said.

'Didn't I tell you that not a whisker of you would be ignored next time?'

'Such audacity! I don't know what to expect of you!' I sat up and put my arms round him. 'Well, you're not going to get a whisker of me, nor the harshest skin on the soles of my feet. You will need to have patience. Patience is virtue and, in the end,' I concluded, 'virtue will be triumphant!'

'Well,' he said with a pretended sigh, 'I suppose our voyage has only begun.'

'Yes, our ship is just sailing out of the harbour.'

'But,' he persisted, 'I see myself as an ambassador, come on board your ship, with costly gifts, seeking an audience!'

'How poetic, but how mischievous! Neil, we really must be getting on our way. Remember we've got to get to Raasay; though I've no doubt you're capable of many more poetic images, once given the reign!'

He persisted in a more serious vein.

'I found it difficult to write to you about sex. The clinical language of textbooks is so impersonal. I'm not overconfident that I'd be successful as a lover, for men have anxieties as well as women. But the joy of success depends on a degree of danger and difficulty.' I could see he was not so shy as I was. 'But in selflessness lies the whole art,' he continued.

'Well, perhaps we could say we've had a fine opening few bars.'

'The prelude,' he added.

'Frills on the dress!' said I.

'A light and airy entrée preceding the main course!'

'Picturesque digressions! Hell's bells, Neil,' I said, 'I'm confounded!' I had exhausted my repertoire. I glanced at my watch. 'Neil,' I said, 'we had better go.'

We hastily threw on our things and made our way to the scooter. As he leapt on he called out, 'Ah, that I could leap into the lady's bed! And you're not just a pretty face.'

It was one of the happiest days of my life, for I had fulfilled all my greatest expectations of myself, as friend, and maybe lover-to-be.

But the 'auspicious gales' we'd hoped for were not to be. After twenty miles of driving we looked for a spot to spend the night and stopped five miles east of Crainlarich, in an open clearing, beside a loch, sheltered by trees which hid us from the road. We did not know it, but we had chosen one of the coldest corridors that runs east to west of the country and we were destined never to leave that spot for four freezing days and nights. Ironically, had we but driven a few miles farther on we would have been back into the sun, but we just stopped short of success.

Winter held that corridor in its icy grip and the weather deteriorated day by day until all sense of playfulness left us, and one miserable incident followed another in one long trail of failure.

Space having been limited on the scooter, it wasn't much of a tent Neil had brought, but we had assembled it then ferried essentials from the scooter near the roadside to the spot we'd chosen. Close by was a small loch and behind us, Ben More.

Snow began to fall. We had no cooker, no fuel and no means of making a hot meal or drink. Neil was exhausted, for he'd travelled from England the day before. We ate poorly, were cramped, and there was nowhere to go. Darkness fell early and, since we had no light, bedtime was to be early too.

Locked into this icy prison was unutterable misery for me, because space and warm bedding were conveniences I required for basic comfort, but there we were in a frail tent, out in a snowfield.

When night came the prospect of sleeping in my clothes did not appeal, and there being no room for manoeuvre in the tent and no desire on my part to undress in these circumstances, I left the tent and went out into the night. Somehow I made my way to the loch to wash in the darkness, but my feet sank into slushy mud. I curtailed that chore. I trudged back towards the tent, where I remembered a clump of bushes. There I tried to undress. My feet sank in bog, and when I lost my balance in the darkness I grabbed a bush, which brought a shower of snow avalanching over my head, shoulders and down my neck. When I returned to the tent I was wetter than when I had left.

Neil was already into his sleeping bag and I crawled miserably into mine.

In the night my body temperature fell sharply and the vibrations from my shivering wakened him.

He sat up, lifted his jumpers and placed my frozen feet against his warm body, then repeated this with my hands until I felt so sorry for him that I tucked myself deep into my bag and forced myself asleep.

In the morning a new fall of snow lay thick upon the ground. We moved around lethargically, for we knew there was no possibility of leaving. Neil tried to light a fire, but the few wreaths of smoke scarcely lifted themselves before dying in the immobilising air. When he suggested we climb Ben More I had no choice but to agree.

We ate sparsely what food we had, dressed in warm clothes, tidied up the tent and left to start the long slog upwards. It was a bright enough day, though snow lay everywhere, but it was marshy on the lower slopes which made walking unpleasant. Then I found the deer fence tricky to get over, and hurt my leg when I jumped off. But Neil was way ahead of me. Just as well, I thought, for sight of him climbing upwards kept me going at a good pace. He stood astride two rocks waving both his arms. His was a small figure in the vastness of the mountain, yet he seemed to me to be tall, strong, able; a giant in his own way. I saw him waiting for me by a stream, mostly frozen over, and I followed him to a gorge, where all shapes and sizes of icicles hung down into it. When he asked me which icicle I wanted, I cheekily pointed to the most inaccessible - intended as a joke - but he decided I was going to have it, and I held my breath to watch him penetrate the dangerous ravine. He had no sooner captured the prize than it slipped from his grasp and went crashing and splintering into the gorge. I settled for a smaller one which I sucked all the way to the top.

Hours passed as we got closer to the summit where the icy covering of the rocks made negotiation difficult. Then we entered an area of deep, soft snow, which travelled up and over the tops of my boots. I was terribly cold and uncomfortable, and my legs were tired and sore. My sole motivation was to see him ahead, knowing that I had to keep going. I'd never cared much for mountain climbing, and the only good thing about this climb was that it passed some of the time in the God-forsaken place. Not that I didn't love Ben More and these mountains, for I did, but I didn't want to be so defeated on my holiday; but I said nothing about it to Neil.

A blizzard was blowing on the final peak and we risked the final climb but only stayed for moments. I was stirred only by the stark and appalling bleakness of snow, peak upon peak, crowding on all sides and into infinite distance; beautiful maybe, but the scene chilled me, for I felt rejected. The mountain did not want us.

Our descent was swift.

We rested for a while in the tent without warmth, without comfort.

Neil insisted we get a hot meal so we set out to walk the five miles to Crianlarich because the scooter had no lights.

After the strenuous climb in the cold and a five mile march, I sensed Neil's spirits were low, which caused me to be dejected. One public bar was the only life on that wintry night in Crianlarich. We entered a large, dimly lit and quite bare room, with dark, chocolate-coloured walls, and never was a place less tempting to enter. We dragged our tired damp bodies to an empty table in a dark corner. Two locals and the barman were the only occupants. I looked up for some inspiration but the nigger-brown walls frowned down on me. Gloom surrounded me and the whole barrenness of the place inflicted a terrible defeat on my spirits, which I had not the will to fight.

A pox on my ignorance for I ordered neither whisky, brandy nor rum, and since there was no food of any kind, nor hot drink, I asked for a ginger beer! I knew no better and no one enlightened me

Neil said nothing and that made me feel tense. We sat there, neither of us saying a word. I wanted so desperately to find my voice. It was an emotional battlefield that required a strategy to win, but in this, I was a noncombatant. My nature was always such that the blight of disappointment shattered any response, devastated the will to fight, and though once or twice about to say something, I didn't, because I felt it better perhaps to say nothing than to say something of such insignificance that it enlarged the banality. And so the words that might have been died on my lips.

The silence grew overwhelming until, at last, one of the men at the bar opened a conversation with the dour barman, nothing of real content, something about vandalism I think, but it provided a mooring for our attention and at once countered the vibes in the gloom. We listened as he talked on, enlarging on his theme, digressing a bit and then concluding his little topic. Because his words gave our minds a focus, I suppose, it imbued what he said with value. Neil commented on how interesting his topic of conversation was, and he was full of praise for it. Now I so desperately wanted that praise, and needed that praise, and it could have been mine if only I'd said things I was earlier prompted to say, but didn't. I sat numb. My feelings spiralled downwards. I think his did too. We soon left.

We had to bend our heads into a blizzard for the five mile journey home, though Neil did put his arms round me to shelter me from the angry 'airt'. There was nothing to redeem another miserable night in the tent.

In the morning, while shaking out my sleeping bag, I was surprised to see two policemen approach. They were asking questions about the scooter. Neil said he would handle the situation and I watched him depart with the policemen. Apparently they took the scooter away for examination too. He looked a bit depressed when he returned. How I wished with all my heart we could have got away, but there was no possibility of that and yet, ironically, though we didn't know it, Valerie and Alistair were at that moment basking in the sunshine of Raasay, wondering where we were.

I tried to gee him along. Lying together in the tent I tried to distract him by asking about his experiences at Craig, which he had once promised to tell me about.

'They have remained a secret. Good. Let there be a veil over many things.'

'And I haven't forgotten that you promised to take me along the ancient bridlepath between Applecross and Sheildaig.'

'And come hell or high water, I will! I promise you! I hope you can be patient, and what's more,' he said, 'I've letters of yours, provoking retaliation and agreement still to answer when I get home. I will keep all my promises. I hope you can wait.'

'But Neil,' I said, 'you won't have so much time now that you're working.'

'Oh Eilidh, you've given me so much of your time. I'm in your debt. I do have more money now, and when we get to the next town, I'm going to buy you a present, to show my appreciation.'

I lay in the tent now with my nose close to the tent flap so that I could flick it open every now and then to see the weather, which at that particular time consisted of big flakes of snow, not soft and fluffy, but with sleet mixed in.

Inevitably, I suppose, Neil spoke sadly as the afternoon wore on and grew grey.

'I've been thinking about this job, Eilidh,' he said. 'I don't know if I can stand a nine-to-five job. You see, I dread the treadmill of repetitiveness.'

Trying to cheer him, I said, 'Maybe you'll be able to work fewer hours.'

'Maybe.'

'Why not just wait and see how it all goes, but I know you really want time to develop your talents.'

Another period of quietness followed before he suggested we walk into Crainlarich and buy some postcards to send home. I agreed, but continued to talk for a little longer.

'You want to send a postcard home?'

'Yes, to my mother.'

'You're fond of your family, aren't you, Neil?'

'I don't know,' he answered surprisingly. 'I sometimes wonder if it's not just an intellectual love I feel for them. When I'm away from them they cease to exist, as if they've passed out of my life.' I had no response to this.

'Some of my college friends have had a warm friendship with my father. He can be delightful company. It has taken me a lifetime to get to know and respect him and appreciate his qualities. By the time my little brother is my age he won't have had a chance to know my father. My father will be dead by that time.'

When he was morose like this my instinct told me to let him talk and that I should play a supportive role. I let him talk.

Snow fell silently outside. Ben More glowered down upon us, winter rebuffed our hopes and paralysed our expectations. There was nothing else to do but talk. And inevitably, too, the topic of the possibility of human happiness returned and extended into a political view.

'We fundamentally differ, you see,' he said. 'I think the human condition is irremediable; I'm sometimes afraid to be happy because I'm afraid of being disillusioned. T.S. Eliot described man as being "incapable of being satisfied with himself, like the peregrine falcon, proud and alone, with no resting place, doomed to wander, to be separate."'

The wind outside gained in strength. My heart went into winter.

'The journey we make through life is endurable because we are advancing towards the compensating destination. The distant goals glitter with allurement, the more wretched our immediate conditions are. But it is not what we had

50

hoped for. Thus I see Marxism, certain tangible remedies are produced like a universal patent pill, to solve all disorders, but I don't believe this will solve the fundamental problems.'

I dreaded the dissertations. I felt like a donkey with boots on trying to chase a butterfly. Of course I admired him for showing an interest in the problems facing mankind but was disappointed that he should always return to the pessimistic reference.

But I argued, 'If our conditions are wretched, then we must strive to improve them and that would at least remove some of the misery, and give us a goal to aim for. But Marxism doesn't pretend that it will cure all ills, only to remedy some of then. Besides,' I continued, 'workers would have a better standard of life, if they owned the means of production.'

'But it wouldn't encourage respect for property or equipment.

'Then there could be marginal deductions for repair and maintenance, but they would still get a greater share of the profits. It would be a fairer system,' I said. 'You would have to agree about that, Neil,' I added with conviction.

He replied to my statement: 'Capitalism places ownership, that is the possibility of great wealth and power in a few hands. Much of the value of their labour is denied them. It becomes excess profit for shareholders, and parasitic speculators. This is a deplorable injustice.'

'I believe that too!'

'It is dangerous. Where power is concentrated, the unscrupulous may exploit it, causing suffering to the many who are unable to resist them.'

'Society,' he continued, 'must advance under socialist planning, for it is less haphazard. Supply will be regulated to demand, no longer subject to artificial fluctuations and planned obsolescence.

'Under world socialism this planning would cover every country. This conception of an economically integrated world brings me back to the question of who will be in control of planning.'

'Well, I suppose there would need to be consultation and discussion,' I said.

'But surely they would lack the comprehensive knowledge necessary. There would have to be adjustments in production for good and bad harvests, fire, flood and so on. Policy would be in the domain of a staff of experts supported by computers and vast statistical services. So there would be no legal freedom for the workers, since the workers could not possibly be aware of the changing circumstances. They would simply have to obey instructions. Without such centralized organisations a co-ordinated industrial and metropolitan world would be impossible, and communism has not prevented the abuse of such concentrated power.'

'But you won't be satisfied with anything short of perfection,' I said.

'I shy away from naïve optimism. The confidence of communism astonishes me, as if a chess pawn should suddenly have the power of a queen but not the knowledge of how to use it; or the knight, from its momentary glimpses of the third dimension, should promulgate a dogmatic theory about it.'

'You accept, then, our present social and political set up?'

'No, I often have harsh feelings combined with pity and perhaps a latent basic sadness that things are as they are. I am no nearer acceptance of our present social and political system. I often feel indifference, mockery and contempt of the figureheads, bosses, wire-pullers and pocket liners. I often feel a hopelessness about the world and myself that things can never be much better. And then I begin to agree with much of what you feel, that only socialism offers a viable solution: at least a fundamental Christian communism.'

Then giving himself a bit of a shake he said, 'Come on, enough of all this theoretical baloney about planning and production while the rain falls and the wind blows, and traffic rumbles along the road. I'm in your debt for listening but I am so dull.'

I was well satisfied with our discussion and he suggested we go to Crianlarich for postcards and to buy some food to eat. We did that, and found it occupied a little more time. For the rest of the day, we idled around for short spells, and every hour or so we passed the time by attempting to light a fire, but no fire would kindle.

Thus, with talking, we cheated a little more time.

The following day there was no let-up in the weather and we repeated everything we'd done the previous day.

'I don't think we'll attempt to go north now,' he said. 'We've lost too much time already.' So we decided to return home the following day.

On our last night he was very quiet. In the tent I snuggled up to him. He whispered, 'Oh Eilidh, I feel I've let you down. I wish for your sake I could be happier.' His voice seemed to call from some abyss of distress.

'But Neil,' I said quietly, 'there is so much for you to be happy about. What is it that you're thinking about? What is it that makes you unhappy?' He drew me closer and whispered, 'I have only one great wish,' he told me, 'and that has been to have less intelligence than I have. You see, I am a victim of my own intelligence. I am at the mercy of talents which make demands on me, and when I try to fulfil these demands, I am not happy. You achieve standards in your mind, which can never be put into practice. I can't do the things I often wish to do because I have to go where my talents lead me. At Cambridge I felt I was a prisoner.'

I could have cried aloud with despair for him. I'd never heard such things before and these were uttered by the only boy in the world I knew I loved.

CHAPTER 7

On my return home I learned that Valerie and Alistair had spent glorious days in sunshine on Raasay, and happily she wasn't too critical of me; indeed, she was in a buoyant mood when she came bouncing into my apartment late one afternoon.

'I've good news,' she said, prancing along the hall on long, elegant legs. Alistair has invited us to Inverness on Saturday. Want to come?'

'Of course, I'd love to,' and I followed her into the living-room.

I could tell from the expression on her face, as she threw herself into an armchair, that she was happy. I put aside the photographs I'd been arranging in the album.

'Well,' she said, playing with a lock of her hair, 'from what I gather of your holiday, you'll be glad of a civilised week-end in Inverness,' she teased, though she never suspected the full disappointment it had been for me. 'I mean,' she continued, 'how could he possibly have expected to get to Raasay on that old scooter! It's not worth anything!'

'It could be said,' I added, 'that we're incorrigible idealists!'

But she wouldn't be brushed aside with a joke.

'Well, I think you're mad, and he's got a cheek to expect you to travel like that! Besides, it's not my idea of a romantic time to get stuck in snow and ice for days on end and have nowhere to go.'

I gave it some moments' thought, before saying dreamily, 'Well, I know it doesn't sound very romantic, Valerie, I suppose it depends on how you define "romantic", but I think it must come in many categories, though for me,' I continued gazing into space, 'I'd travel a thousand miles just to be where he is, and when I hear his name, my mind trails off into a daydream slumber.'

'Well then,' she said, quite unmoved by this, 'you must be the oddball!'

'I, the oddball!' I countered. 'Don't be so fanciful, Valerie. Very little in this world will ever bear the stamp of my signature on it. I haven't enough character for that. And don't forget, I didn't choose him. He crossed my path.'

'Oh well, I suppose so. But he's certainly full of surprises.'

'I know that. If he were suddenly to pull out a catherine wheel from behind his left ear, in the midst of distinguished company, I wouldn't be surprised!'

I started to clear away books and papers from the table to make way for the tray, but she had started me on a train of thought. I paused for a moment.

'You know, Valerie, he's a strange sort of person,' and I stopped what I was so purposefully doing, and sat down. 'When I can talk to you like this, it helps me to understand things better. There's more to him than meets the eye. On the surface, you can tell he's intellectual, and therefore you expect him to command the confidence that goes with it; but when I uncover that layer, I find vulnerability, and if I peel that away, I find a humility that acknowledges others' worth but refuses to acknowledge his own. He has a rare sort of feeling for people and maybe someday he will be able to write about them with conviction.' And on that conclusion, I rose once more and prepared the small table for some tea.

She sat, saying nothing, elbow on the arm of the chair, not even pretending an interest, for she was honest. I spread the teacloth then continued, 'If you could only be bothered listening to me a bit more, Valerie,' I said, and she nodded her consent, 'I'll tell you what worries me most.' I spoke slowly and deliberately, as I ordered my thoughts. 'When he's happy and in buoyant mood, he carries me along with him. But if he's feeling low, and things have not been going well for him, then I just dry up. I have nothing to say.' Then I added with more emphasis, 'I don't seem to be able to follow on with my own contribution. It seems such clap-trap after what he's just said. Do you know what I mean? He's so cultured, that's the problem, and I just seem to fumble. Honestly Valerie, I can't tell you how stupid I feel. It's awful.' And before she could interrupt I continued, 'After he has spoken, I'm still fumbling for words, and suddenly there's a big space, and the silence is so conspicuous. And I just stand there as if I were on the edge of a deep pool and I want to throw in a penny hoping for a ripple or two, but really expecting it to drop to the bottom in silence.'

'Hmmm,' she yawned. 'I just think you make a fuss about nothing.'

'I get so embarrassed, Valerie.'

'I wouldn't bother about it if I were you.'

'Sometimes it's all right, you know,' I persisted, 'but then sometimes the silence is so conspicuous. It was like that at Crianlarich. A lot of the time I just said nothing. Val, I'm dreading a letter. I'm sure he'll say I'm a bore!'

'You worry too much,' she replied shrugging her narrow shoulders. 'I wouldn't give a damn if I were you!' and she got up to stretch her legs and play with the cat, while I went to fetch the tea.

Soon I returned and we sat there eating sandwiches as I recalled how she did not perform to advantage when she wanted to impress a boyfriend because she, too, became tense and her natural charm was lost, but I could never tell her that.

'By the way,' she said, helping herself to another sandwich, 'it's just occurred to me to ask if he has any idea of how you feel about him.'

'Well, I don't write pages of purple prose if that's what you mean. I just tell him things that happen, or assert an opinion, pull his leg, tell him off . . . that sort of thing. You remember what Dr Johnson said to the woman who kept showering him with compliments: "Consider what your praise is worth, Madame, before you choke me with it." Don't worry, Valerie, I show him in lots of ways how I care for him. Besides, he's more poetic towards me than I am to him.'

I rose to fill the teapot so that she wouldn't see the secret smile on my face to recall the first poem he ever sent me:

'From far from eve and morning,
And you twelve-winded sky,
The stuff of life to knit me
Blew hither, here am I.

Now for a while I tarry,
Nor yet disperse apart,
Take my hand quick and tell me
What have you in your heart?

Speak now and I will answer.
How can I help you say?
Ere to the winds twelve quarters
I take my endless way.'

When I returned I suggested we change the subject and I opened the window for some cool, fresh air.

'Anyway, remind me to plunder my wardrobe for something nice to wear for going to Inverness on Saturday.'

At the mention of 'Inverness' her face took on a more serious cast. 'I wonder if he'll have other friends there,' she said ruefully.

Alistair spent so much of his time round other people it could be disconcerting, especially for Valerie, who was fond of him.

'It's just because he's so friendly, Val, and remember, that's why we like him.'

'Yes, that's true,' she said, somewhat pacified. 'You think he's a bit shallow, don't you?' though she wasn't at all sure that I did.

'A bit vain, maybe, but that's all.'

'Don't you think there's a bit more to him than that?' she persisted.

'Oh yes, there's a lot more to him than that,' I assured her.

'I've often tried to put my finger on the attraction, Valerie. For me, it's something about his gait, the way he strides out, as if going to meet the world that is there to welcome him, with the offer of good things. It's like an infection, I've always thought. You catch the joy of life from him . . . something like that.'

'Yes, that's right, but then again, don't you think it's also because they feed his ego, that he goes out to welcome them?'

'People wouldn't feed his ego unless they liked him, Val, and it's his joy of living that attracts them, and they just return his warmth. He's used to being liked and he expects it. What I wonder is whether, if he met someone who didn't like him, it wouldn't turn him sour. That's where I don't have so much confidence.'

'Do you find him attractive, though? You've said you like him so I suppose you do, and you've known him for longer than I.'

Valerie was beginning to feel out my relationship with Alistair and it was time for me to put her at ease.

'Yes, I knew him long before you, that's true. And yes, I could look forward to a happy life with Alistair and an intellectually comfortable life, because I think we are fairly well matched. I laugh at the same things he does, and I'm at ease with his friends, and like him; I get on well with people.' At this juncture I could see her head give the little tilt it did when she was perplexed or ill at ease, so I continued, marking every word with emphasis.

'Of course, Alistair and I could never have a future together,' and I gave that a second to sink in before continuing. 'He could never be right for me, nor I for him.' Slowly spreading the gospel of peace I added, 'For one thing, I don't have a religious background, though I've always believed that men are my brothers and the world is my country, but we're not drawn together in that meaningful, religious way. Nor do I have the social graces that would be desirable.

'For example, I once made a memorable exhibition of myself. I was having lunch with Alistair at the Theological College in Edinburgh and found myself at a long table in the refectory, sitting opposite a row of very sober-looking gentlemen, who fidgeted with embarrassment. When the soup was served, one gent offered me a piece of white bread, which I had the boldness to reject in preference to what I believed to be brown bread, only to discover I'd lifted a piece of gingerbread! It was as if all the serious faces stopped eating at once to stare, and, as usual with me, I couldn't handle the situation, so I just continued to eat the gingerbread with mortification and neither Alistair nor I ever mentioned the incident.'

She chuckled.

'Oh I thought that would please you!' I laughed, and was glad of her sense of humour. At times like that, she seemed vulnerable, but it gave her an air of femininity and, if her nature wasn't all sweetness, she had a basic goodness that could not engage dislike and I mused that Alistair, with his love of life, would carry her along the road to a future of full-blown happiness, but Neil's self-doubt and depression would have buried her joy of living. But I felt some time would have to pass before Alistair would feel able to settle down.

The week-end duly came and Alistair smilingly welcomed us in crisp shirt, flannels and loose sweater, a total picture of comfort, well-being and bonhomie.

He occupied a Victorian house on the banks of the River Ness. He ushered us in to a white-painted parlour of dainty elegance. A rosewood bookcase of small proportions occupied one corner, beside an exotic climbing plant; in another, a writing desk, with a tidy top; a rather battered sofa occupied the centre of the room and over-looked the garden, full of roses. Photographs, ornaments and exotic pieces gave a homely air to the room, and a cream carpet lit it up with brightness.

Afternoon tea was served with all the silver accoutrements and pleasantries associated with the activity.

Conversation was easy, gay and intermittent.

I wanted Alistair and Valerie to spend the rest of the day together and so I insisted on staying in, to sample more of the grandeur of living in this charming Victorian house with the rose garden; a wish readily granted, and so I sat with my own thoughts for the rest of the afternoon.

On Sunday, we three walked by the river towards the Cathedral. I declined to go into the Cathedral with them, however, allowing them their private time together, and watched them disappear through the ancient heavy doors.

I returned along the riverbank in leisurely fashion, glancing across at the Cathedral, standing in solitary splendour, filling me with inspiration as a shaft of sunlight lit up its golden stone. I wished the best and most for my two friends, and then I thought of Neil, whose invisible companionship took me through the doors of my own 'cloud-capped towers and gorgeous palaces!'

But later that day we had to say farewell to Alistair. I knew Valerie would be feeling miserable. We always did when we left someone behind whom we loved or had feelings for, and of course, for the pleasures gone.

We always had difficulty cheering each other up, but generally what we found worked for us was to tuck in and have a binge, a sort of death by overeating. 'Let's have a binge, Valerie,' I said, after she'd driven for some time without saying anything.

'The sooner the better,' she said darkly.

'Dates and chocolate.'

'No, fish and chips.'

'Right, dates and chocolate in the car at Aviemore; fish and chips in the rain at a street corner in Pitlochry.'

'Done.'

And we survived!

CHAPTER 8

I waited for acknowledgement of the Easter disaster. My God, how I dreaded the letter. I wondered what words he would pen in response to that awful experience. Of that, I could not guess.

My trembling fingers opened the letter when at last it came; I read with disbelief: No death blow.

'I think of us climbing Ben More,' he wrote, 'and always with tender and vivid memories, one of the great days of my life, our life, since you are inseparable from it.'

Thus he started. So out of the dreary memory of wintry paralysis, something of life stirred, an ember of the experience which he fanned into life, or a flower plucked from the weeds. There was for me something deeply moving, and typically so, about his sensitive desire to sift from the dross of it, a powdering of gold. I felt profound gratitude. He went on:

'I remember the shivering saplings of pine on the lower slopes, that massive icicle I failed to capture for you that hung over a glassy abyss of ice; the magnificent upper slopes; the snow packed firm underfoot and the fitful gusts whirling the surface "dust" into spirals that stung our faces as they blew by the cornices of the ridge, and the dissociation from place and time, when we breasted the huge wind, shielding our skin from its bite, and peering into a sort of obscure cauldron of dizzy-billowing cloud – and the momentary revelation of miles of uncoloured mountain, through a wanly lit sunlit cleft in the cloud. Inextinguishable memory!'

So, all was not lost, after all. I still had cause to hope. And nothing daunted, he invited me to Cambridge! 'What the hell!' I burst out, overwhelmed with relief, 'he's asked me!'

He wants me! I'm going! I'll get dolled up! Val can advise me. I'll wear my bright green, cotton frock, with splashes of white daisies, high heels, and designer accessories! I'll show him!

Valerie was putting the finishing touches to my nails. 'Pity you're going by bus,' she remarked a little sadly. 'You'll have to sit rather stiffly all night so as not to crush your clothes.'

'Well, the train's out of the question Valerie. I can't afford such a luxury.

And I don't care, for I'm going to have a great time. I can't wait Val. I'm all a flutter!'

'Keep still!' she implored.

'Wait till he sees me, Val. I'll be a splash of colour, a streak of sunlight, a star falling out of dreary Scottish skies and lighting up the Fens!'

'Cambridge,' exclaimed Val. 'here she comes to conquer!'

I travelled overnight to Peterborough arriving early in the morning, where I was to change buses. Emerging from the bus, I noticed to my horror that my gorgeous dress was horribly crushed. I had sat upright most of the night but must have dozed off for moments and there was the result. In anguish I said to myself, 'I can't go. I can't meet him like this!' Typically, misery swallowed me up. To think I'd built up my confidence as one cultivates a rare plant, only to have it perish on the threshold of its bloom.

I shook myself and sped down the road frantically looking for a laundry, but it was still early morning and only the street market was turning to. I rushed here and there and everywhere until I found a laundry. What luck! The lady had just unpadlocked the door and I rushed rudely into the shop.

'Can you launder a dress for me?' I gasped.

She continued opening up . . . first the blinds, then the till, put on her overall, tied it in a tidy bow, then replied nonchalantly. 'Yes, I can launder it.' Magic! I glanced at my watch to see how much time I had.

'When will it be ready?'

'You can have it next Thursday!'

I backed out of the shop as if I were in a maze of madness, my eye still rivetted upon the woman. Once in the street again I tried to gather my wits, but as I instinctively made my way towards the bus I glanced down and saw that the damp early morning air was ironing out the creases in my dress.

I boarded the bus and before long, it was pulling into the station at Cambridge. I spotted him at once emerging from the corner, instantly recognisable by his nervous vitality and jaunty step, his face radiating pleasure. Why I bothered about my dress I don't know. Had I been meeting Alistair and arrived crinkled, his sense of glamour would have been outraged; but this was Neil, who would see all in one camera flash and open his arms and welcome me with joy.

And I couldn't believe my eyes. He was wearing a suit! I'd never seen him dressed in anything other than loose ex-army jackets, and his heavy walking boots. He came towards me now, nervously fingering his tie, gave me a hug and a kiss, took my bag and whisked me off. I was in a bit of a flutter myself and, to allay my embarrassment, I commented on the tie he was wearing for I'd given it to him for a present.

'Oh, you noticed!' he smiled, steering me round a corner. 'You've rather spoiled me with presents, you know.'

As we walked briskly along the road, he turned to look at me again and said, 'How is it you look younger every time I see you?'

'It must be the company I keep or the correspondence I receive,' I quipped.

'We haven't far to go,' he said. 'I'm just round the corner from the bus station.'

I noticed then the name of the street I addressed my mail to. He breezed along the pavement at a brisk pace, I clattered along in my high-heeled shoes beside him, stealing glances from the corner of my eye, and noticing fine shoes and smart suit and shirt.

We had been walking along a narrow street in front of a row of terraced houses and now he stopped at a plain little door. He started fumbling in his pocket for his key until I had begun to think he'd lost it in his excitement. I stood there for what felt like ages and seemed to see every little thread-like crack in the painted door, until at last, after some scary fidgeting, he retrieved it, and I was led into a tiny scullery which in turn led into a small, square living-room. I looked for a place to lay my coat but then he took my things and disappeared into an adjoining room with them. I heard him bustling around, which gave me time to gather some poise, for I was always afraid of being bombarded by his wit and losing my own. I felt like Alice in Wonderland in the miniature room. Neil returned and, standing in front of me asked, 'Well, what do you think?' he asked, moving a little anxiously from one foot to the other.

'This house is so small and dainty, so spick and span, so neat and clean,' I said, realising he'd been working hard. 'It's just a delight!' He was pleased with that.

'Now tell me what you *really* think' he said, still smiling.

'What I really think . . . ? Well, let me see . . . now that you've given me *carte-blanche*. Well, it's not exactly extravagantly furnished or dominated by luxury.' Then I looked around the room. There was a small table that stood on skinny legs and two spindly chairs that a puff of wind from the not-too-strong-looking window would have blown over, a settee of doll-like proportions, with an old shapeless blanket thrown over it, and a small electric fire in the hearth, but no picture or ornament to adorn in any way.

'I mean . . .' I said, attempting humour, '. . . It needs a spot of colour, some extravagance to make a bolder statement in the room, to take away from the drabness.'

'Like what?' he challenged.

'Well, a nice bright throw-over would enliven that drab settee,' I said, making my point and smiling.

'But,' he protested, 'I'm told I haven't the best taste in the management of "throw-overs".

'I'm joking Neil. It's all I could have wished for, spartan though it is.'

'I promise I will try to achieve something more elaborate for your next visit.'

'Perhaps something of flamboyant French taste?'

'Perhaps . . . or of Baroque grandeur. And I'll try to remember to display my collection of Imari or Chinese plate. Will that do?'

'I'm more interested in China cups than Chinese plate,' I laughed, and off he darted into the scullery, where I soon heard the rattle of teacups.

'It's not luxurious,' he called through to me, 'but it's all I need and I'm lucky to have it.'

I moved to the scullery door. 'Yes, it's a place of your own.' He soon emerged with the tea-tray and we sat down at the table.

'Thanks for meeting me off the bus, Neil,' I said, as he poured the tea.

Then, looking up with a gleam in his eye, said, 'Well, you know, only death or chronic diarrhoea would have kept me from meeting you,' and he gave a muted guffaw, before I helped myself to a sandwich, which he'd prepared for us. Glancing mischievously at me again, he continued, 'Or catching my most treasured member in that ramshackle window,' and he lifted the tea-pot and filled my cup.

I solemnly shook my head.

'Do you remember *Tristram Shandy*?' he resumed.

I nodded, for he'd recommended that I read it.

'The boy's nurse instructs him to piss out of an upstairs window, but the window is hanging by a thread, and it crashes down and deflowers him,' said he, buttering his bread and roguishly smiling. 'It deflowers him in the middle of the act, in mid-piss, as it were . . . do you remember that bit?' he asked with more laughter.

'I do,' said I, helping myself to another sandwich. 'I was surprised that a vicar had written it.'

'Yes, Lawrence Sterne wrote it, a masterpiece of comic description, so, if you sense that I ever tremble on the verge of such a relief, that I'm about to disgrace my noble lineage, a line of Celtic chieftains, who never pissed but in a proper place, God bless their propriety, if you fear this . . .' he continued, '. . . seize me by the shoulder, spin me round and cry out, "Remember Tristram".'

'Once you get the bit between your teeth, Neil, there's no stopping you,' I said. 'Are you sure you're sober?'

'Oh, I knew you would be appalled.'

'And I thought I knew you, so now I see your real self . . . a scumbag!'

63

'You didn't know I was a pornographer of Rabelaisian proportions?'

'Oh, I had a good idea that people of your education are well versed in that!'

'Anyway, *you* can't talk' he said.

'What do you mean?'

'You once told me that one of your favourite sounds was a cow pissing.'

'Yes, I love cows and everything about them, especially the way they stand and stare.'

'Yes,' he said, pouring more tea, 'if you stand and look at the cow as she pisses, she carries on steadfastly with an air of dour impudence, gazing at you from under lowered lids. It's so fierce, downright and unequivocal, this in a cow. She does it with emphatic completeness, then resumes her chewing and cropping.'

'Well,' I interrupted, 'before I give you a look of dour impudence, could I have another sandwich?' He passed the plate.

When a shaft of sunlight suddenly shot through the window, I remarked on the beautiful day and asked what we were going to do.

'Well, I'm going to show you the city,' he said, and added shyly, 'and I'm going to buy you a present.' A quick freshen up and we were gone.

We visited Fitzwilliam Museum, examining some of the paintings, giving criticisms here and appreciations there, Neil's comments generally being humorous, but neither of us knew much about art. We continued to the university and, while walking through it – for Neil hoped to locate a friend working in the science faculty – I sensed that he grew, not uneasy exactly, but his gait slowed down and he became noticeably meditative, and I suggested we did not stay long. Having located his academic friend and exchanged pleasantries, we left and eventually arrived at Heffers bookshop.

In Heffers, I teased him that he almost ran amok. I was left an orphan in the corner of the shop while he handled lovingly books on almost every shelf, with an interest so intense he didn't mind pushing his way through. To my delight, he quite 'lost' himself, and while I watched him with curiosity, I indicated I was in no hurry to go.

He was in danger of losing his composure, I told him when he came out.

'This is for you,' he said, presenting me with a book. My smile said it all.

We made our way towards the park. We walked slowly now, he, composed and superior, I, timid and worshipping. 'You know,' he said, taking my hand in his, 'my conscience troubles me, for I haven't replied to your last letter yet.'

'Neil, I've far more time than you.'

'You know you outdo me in your letter-writing.'

'And you outdo me in your tape-recordings,' I said.

'Yes, I've been listening to a lot of Shakespeare's plays and taping them, so we'll have an infinite chest of spiritual riches.'

'Yes, and we must have music too,' I said.

'Of course,' he went on. 'It's not to prefer art to life and escape to it, returning with contempt to life, but to absorb it, as an interpretation, an ordered and coherent comment on, and enrichment of life to recognise in what happens to, in and around us the scattered fragments of the greatest poems and plays, pieces waiting to be shaped and fitted.'

Mention of the future gave me cause for hope. We entered the gates of the park and I indicated a bench and we sat down. He threw nuts to the squirrels.

'Are you happy with your teaching, Neil?' I asked. 'How's it going?'

'I can't say I'm happy with it,' he said, turning to look at me. 'Teaching is a limitless task and, being such, I can't put it out of my mind.'

I recognised the old Neil in the 'old' territory.

'It frets and exhausts me,' he said, throwing small handfuls of nuts.

'But everyone who teaches feels that,' I insisted. 'Besides, I can't believe your work to be anything other than very competent,'

'But I'm always looking for perpetual, glowing radiance, not fleeting glimpses,' he said.

When a couple approached the bench with a dog, we moved off through the park, walking slowly, with my arm through his.

'Neil' I said, 'you'll have to try and be satisfied with less.' He thought for a moment before he answered.

'You see,' he explained, 'I don't really want competent mediocrity. I know you'll think that a dreadfully unkind dismissal of thousands of honest workers – believe me, I don't mean it to be – but the even performance of worthwhile work doesn't attract me.' When he drew me closer I rested my head on his shoulder.

'But Neil,' I said, trying to be helpful, 'those who don't achieve brilliance in their work don't have disastrous failures either, and one has to be grateful for that. Will that not do for you too?'

After a moment's reflection, he said, 'No. I prefer the hazardous unknown. I don't want an even journey across a plain. I want a peak or a pit, a wire trembling with high potential, stretching across an abyss . . . you see,' and he turned to face me, 'it's this which allures me.'

I swallowed hard. How strange he was. To face the unknown would be a nightmare.

'Let's sit here for a moment,' I said, 'before we go home.'

'We're not going home' he said to my surprise. 'I'm taking you out to dinner,' and he squeezed my hand, but we sat down again. I never liked it when he said sad things and I wanted to continue the dialogue in the hope his outlook might be brighter.

'But if the hazardous unknown attracts you. Neil,' I persisted, 'and also impairs your energy, what then?' I looked down at my feet as though I had a great burden on my shoulders.

'Then I get tired,' he said, 'and I don't want to face the world,' and he turned to me and took my face in his hands and said, 'Oh, Eilidh, don't let it worry you. I can salvage a little respect for myself. The whole me isn't the tired, withdrawn depressive one. There is a deeper self, and though it's often extinct, when I'm with you for example, I know that it exists, and then I've cause for hope. It's just *how* to nourish and strengthen this vital core.'

I suggested we go and eat, for I wanted this sad bit of conversation to end. Neil gathered up his books saying, 'You must think I'm a hopeless case. I often feel hopeless when I face the world.' As we walked away, he added, 'But don't worry, Eilidh, it's not the only reality.' I hugged him.

He went on, 'I'm sure it's not the only reality . . . feeling hopeless, I mean; one glimpses it, touches it. Grace and sin are the theological terms, the light and the dark . . . I wonder if they are neutral, tacit prisoners, co-existing in animate things, awaiting release in animate man, in whom they battle for supremacy.' I said nothing but felt like a sheep that couldn't bleat.

Eating out was at least without all those lugubrious conversations, and I felt more light-hearted when we returned home.

'Get the kettle on, Neil,' I called, as he disappeared with my jacket, and I kicked off my shoes. 'Might as well make myself at home,'

He pulled the sofa over to the hearth.

'We could listen to the music, Neil, if you like, I said, as I sat down with my back against the sofa.

'I'm afraid I've taken all my equipment home,' he replied. 'You know me, I'm always in need of transport,' he smiled. handing me my mug of tea.

'Anyway,' he added, 'if I'd been listening to a symphony, I might well have relapsed into a mood of irresponsible euphoria and there's no telling what I might say . . .'

'There's no telling what you might say at *any* time,' I said with some authority.

He sat down beside me. There wasn't much heat from his fire but there was a pleasant stillness outside and the time slipped away, and he was relaxed. I'd noticed that when he was in a relaxed mood he was happy to let me do the talking.

'Do you like living in Cambridge, Neil? Does it suit you?'

'Well . . . yes. I know the city well, you see, and I can use the facilities of the university library for private research.'

'What research would you like to do, then?' I wondered.

'The contributions to English literature of writers and poets of Celtic and Gaelic origin.' And he gave me a sidelong glance as if to say, 'I wonder if she'll believe me'. And I gave him a meaningful look.

'When I applied for the job anyway, that was one of the reasons I gave.'

'And that's what you want to do?'

'Well,' he said dissembling, 'it's not a complete fabrication, though respectably distant from what I believe the truth to be at this moment.' I got the smile of mischief I was expecting.

'I can read your mind, you know; you've less surprises for me than you once had.'

'Actually, I had an idea for a book this morning, an adaptation of *David Copperfield* suitable for non-academic classes.'

'You and your ideas . . . you're so prolific.'

'Yes,' he laughed, 'it's just in their execution that I'm defeated!'

'I hope you manage to work some humour into your teaching . . . with your imagination it shouldn't be difficult.'

'Yes, as a matter of fact I do. I often introduce stories and jokes into my lesson, shamelessly proclaiming their irrelevance! Then I quote from newspapers or from Shakespeare or even my own dreams, and I begin at the end of the lesson and work backwards, the "Irish" method I tell them! It keeps the class alive to the unexpected. In this way you can practise the theatrical or showman side of teaching and maintain the friendliest atmosphere consonant with an unmistakably earnest emphasis on intellectual and linguistic rigour.'

'And you're the most popular teacher in the school?'

'Yes!'

'Go on. Make me another cup of tea, Neil, and when you're on your feet bring me another cushion for my back.'

It was growing late and when he put his arm round my shoulder, I snuggled up close to him. After a few moments of stroking my shoulder he said, with a sly, sidelong look, 'I'm not altogether happy.'

'Happy about what?'

'I'm not altogether happy stroking your shoulder.'

I sensed mischief. 'Well, you lecherous devil, you can stroke my satin skirt.'

'Oh,' he sighed, 'it's too smooth, but I have a faint perversion in caressing a garment and not you.'

'Yes,' I giggled, 'I suspected you were a pervert! Anyway, I resent such bare-faced physical advances,' I added, responding to his mischief.

'You know ... something you said in your last letter made my breast tremble,' said he, continuing the farce.

'That's an excuse, Neil,' I said, but feeling I must needs be daring too, I said, 'And was that all that trembled?'

'No,' he replied. 'I felt a sort of quivering about the lower vertebrae.'

'I'm sure I don't command such letter-writing techniques,' I said.

'I felt an eager striving potency between the thighs.'

'Oh, stop, Neil, please! Don't reveal all!'

'Oh, I won't! Total revelations are so shocking! They leave nothing more to hope for, to speculate about. The supreme artist reveals a little, then a little more as the impulse prompts, but he always keeps something in reserve.'

There was no stopping him, and he referred, and not for the first time, to his 'most treasured member'.

'He's trembling already,' he continued, 'at the thought of extended service to his mistress. Be assured he's in marvellous condition, fit for public parade and exhibition!

'Neil! Where's your sense of dignity!'

'But my treasure is not to be counted mine alone. Didn't I say that treasures shared are treasures doubled?' he continued, nothing daunted.

To steal a moment from my embarrassment, I loosened the velvet bow on my hair and let it hang loose, but he went on.

'Such a caressing power in this trunk of strange virtue, smooth and straight and rising to the touch as nothing else in nature. It is of itself incomplete, needing another to share, but of this,' he said softly, 'I can say no more.'

'I can't return your poetry, Neil, but are you inviting me to enter paradise a while?'

'I am.'

It wasn't Neil I was unsure of, but myself. He was an intellectual colossus that towered above me. For him, everything we did together was a memorable occasion, a high adventure, a unique experience, to be recalled and relished; and because in my heart of hearts, I knew he was a prize beyond my dreams, my shyness and tension could not be released. I told him only that I was too shy.

'I hope you don't resent it Neil,' I said sadly.

'How could I?' he replied. 'You've declined so gracefully. I just felt that everything seemed so propitious, but I respect you the more.'

I was grateful for his acceptance and manliness, and I did feel deeply sorry for him. But before night enfolded us in sleep, we lay together, arms entwined, in one long, tight embrace.

'I'm going to kiss you,' he whispered, 'till I'm exhausted . . . on one condition . . . you kiss me till you're exhausted! And woe be to him who first cries, "Hold".'

I knew I'd salvaged a little happiness for him, and before I closed my eyes in sleep, I thought of one of Chaucer's characters, the 'Verray gentile, parfitt knighte'. But I was not happy with myself. I was denying a fine young man whom I dearly loved, a pleasure he was entitled to expect.

Next morning I awoke to the smell of toast. I quickly washed, dressed, breakfasted and gave my compliments to the chef.

'You've been an impeccable host, Neil.'

'Oh, must you go home today?'

'Of course I must. I've got school tomorrow.'

He was reluctant to let me go.

'Do you think you'll never see me again, or what?'

The time to leave had come.

However unequal this partnership, I wasn't going to run away from it, but one of the dangers I faced with him was being confronted by the unexpected, which would trigger a panic in this heart now so intimately tuned to every nuance of feeling, now so much in dread of discord where it had heard only harmony before, because I was so insecure about this relationship. One of these destructive moments was about to bear down on me.

My bags had been packed early to allow for a last minute chat or even that last cup of tea or lingering farewell.

I was having a last look out of the window, when Neil came over beside me.

'I'm so glad you've been happy this week-end,' he said, and he took my arm and asked me to sit on the sofa with him.

He spoke quietly. 'Some years ago, I was convinced that there was only one ideal partner for every man and woman. Now I rather feel that for only a few is such an ideal possible . . . the most must accept a compromise of partner, of which there may be many.'

My heart raced. *What* is *he going to say?*

'I know I'm not handsome, or muscular or physically commanding, so I appreciate that many women would quickly pass me by; that is, you could easily find someone more obviously stimulating.'

I grew stiff with tension. I felt consternation. I looked down and hung my head as a victim does at the time of execution, all life suspended, except the panicking heart, awaiting the blow to fall.

'I cannot tell you how much I could come to love you in time,' he continued.

Oh what's coming?

69

'You're so wilfully self-effacing; you deny your own qualities, or overvalue intellect or wit against gentleness, loyalty and affection. Don't. There are many women more beautiful, more seductive, more graceful than you. Perhaps if I sought such a woman I might win her. I don't wish to.'

There's bad news coming I thought. My heart thumped, but I did not move.

'Grace and intelligence are not deceitful,' he said, 'but where the outer elegancies are most developed, the possible inner nullity is the more effectively disguised. I think I'm the average compromise case.' And here he paused, probably sensing the hushed silence beside him.

He looked at me and said, 'You're probably discovering the faults for yourself that I've warned you of. I want you to remember that you're not bound to me if you wish to break away.'

What's he saying . . . a veiled warning?

'If you feel someone else might make you happier, then you must feel free to break away.'

I was stunned, speechless.

'Don't take this unkindly,' he said. 'I'm only trying to see the truth and say it,' he continued, holding my hand.

I didn't want to hear the truth. I didn't want to hear any more. I just wanted to be home again.

'Oh, Eilidh,' he said, 'don't drop your head like that.' With a gentle hand he lifted my head.

'Take me to the bus, now,' I said quietly. 'I must get home.'

I tried to be brave. I thanked him for his hospitality.

Before he saw me on to the coach, he called. 'I know it's arrogant of me, but I'm absolutely sure that you don't wish to break away from me.'

During the long journey home I managed, by degrees, to work the alarm out of my system by poring over every statement he'd made and every word he'd spoken. Finally I came to the conclusion that he was simply offering me a freedom to find someone else if I found he wasn't, after all, the man of my dreams.

It took me a long time to solve because, as my heart always took over my head, my emotion was difficult to control, and the encounter made me aware of the strength of my involvement and the frailty of a heart ready to shatter at the merest whisper of failure.

At the same time, I realised I would have to look to my own faults. I knew Neil was disappointed that there had been no sexual encounter, and I decided to take this to the battlefield.

I went to the doctor and he told me I was physically all right. I went to the nurse and she told me how to relax. One lunchtime I left school and went to the local corner shop.

'A bottle of gin, please,' I asked.

I hid it in my basket underneath some fruit. That night, in the privacy of my room, I would experiment. I'll learn fast, I said to myself. And I did my best.

Very shortly after this, an invitation came from Neil. He was unexpectedly going to be in Scotland on an errand for a friend and offered to meet me, and we'd go to the Yorkshire moors on Saturday and he'd return me on the Sunday, and I readily agreed.

'We'll go to the forest,' he wrote, 'and find a warm and sunny hollow, and we'll make love as we've never made love before.'

I could return confidently, 'We'll have a day of fire and feeling . . . a day to remember always.'

But that was to be a hollow dream.

He collected me in a storm of heavy winter rain and the journey on the scooter became an abominable experience. Lorries showered us with slush, for snow had fallen on the high ground. We were forced to make a stop in the town and buy more waterproofs, as the ones I wore had already been torn to shreds by high winds. We were drenched many times over. The vexatious scooter had to be pushed so often, it became an exhausting experience for both of us. I never knew a human frame could shiver so much. We were losing stamina. Neil took us off the road and tried to recover under trees, and once we got under the trees, snow came sliding off and piled on top of us, then ran down our necks. I was so astonished at the amount of punishment we had taken that I actually burst out laughing.

'It's not human to be so good-natured as you,' he said. Although he was solemn, he did nestle in and try to comfort me while water began to fill up in my shoes.

The promise had been to spend the afternoon in the woods and we had arrived after many hours, but we had not anticipated this weather. I didn't like to say anything, but the plan should have been aborted.

But Neil was solemn. We reached the moors and parked the scooter and he walked as if hell-bent on a journey of annihilation. Rain continued to fall. Neil was silent. Had he been cheerful, I would have reflected his cheerfulness, but he was sullen too. He must have been exhausted, with the long drive from England to Scotland and back again. A blanket of silence descended. Sensing the solemnity, I dried up. Neither of us spoke. Mentally and physically we were in a state of fatigue, so there could be little hope for our emotions. Flagging and wearied, we laboured on. Why did we not turn back? We were hurting each other with this taciturnity. I absorbed despondency like a sponge. These were the grimmest moments I can every remember. I longed to break the silence but my lips wouldn't move. Raw drops of rail fell around us, hung languidly round the neck of every forest grass, hung in grey beads from the forest fences and fell from the trees as we passed underneath. Why did we plod on? Why did we further stain the dark atmosphere with such insensibility? Mud smacked under our feet and the silent march went on.

I moved my lips and managed, 'Curse this weather, Neil,' and, trying again, added, 'I didn't expect this.'

With a forlorn air, he said, 'I wanted it to be warm and fine.'

Eventually it seemed even the heavens had had enough, and the cloud broke at last, emitting a shaft of sparse sunlight, wan though it was but in a sort of way cheering us with the hope of more to come.

'Let's call a halt and find a sunny spot to lie in, he said, but not with any enthusiasm. We found a clearing.

'Let's rest while there's a little sun,' I said. It was tearfully obvious that neither of us was happy. He sat a little apart from me, which I felt was symbolic of the emotional distance between us, and I was at the bottom of a spiral of decline.

'It's not pleasure for me to sit apart from you, Neil,' I said, adjusting my position. The atmosphere between us was heavy as clay.

Attempting a lightness of tone, he replied, 'And you might torment me with your nearness.' But it seemed to me that his heart was not in what he said.

Then he added sadly, 'And I had hoped we might make love.'

'And we will,' I said.

'But,' he protested, 'are you not reluctant?'

'No.'

'Are you only acquiescing to what I want in order to keep me happy?'

'No.'

But I knew in my heart that I had lied. This was not the time and the place. I was wet, miserable, cold, exposed, uncomfortable, exhausted and deeply unhappy, and he must have felt as I did. I could only conclude that he hoped to salvage something worthwhile from a flawed and failed week-end.

'I'll be an artist for you,' he said, but from his tone, his heart was not there. 'I'll be courteous and patient.'

We lay there for a while until the motionless, brooding atmosphere of the wet forest eloquently declared defeat. Though Neil, indeed, was courteous, not only was nothing of success achieved, nor any good salvaged, but also it endowed the occasion with a special stamp of failure, which even the elements sensed, as rain drew a curtain of despair over the blighted scene.

We rose and walked away. Like soldiers returning from defeat, we plodded solemnly back to where we'd left the scooter, stale, flat and frigid. At least at the end of battle one can have a bath, a hot meal and a good night's sleep.

We at last arrived at the spot where we had left the scooter . . . but it was gone!

We looked about. Neil concluded that the police must have taken it. Now we were stranded, miles from anywhere. If we had spoken little before, we said even less now. Grimly, with lips tight and jaws set, we started to walk along an open road, with fields on either side. Some long time later, a car approached and offered us a lift. Neil made an effort to speak to these two nice people, but I grew sullen. They dropped us off at the Police Station, but not before one final spectacle of wretchedness, when, as Neil got out of the car, his foot caught in the seat belt and he clumsily tumbled on to the pavement. I stood in silence, looking on at the scene of indignity, and silence completed this totality of misery. There was no anger between us, just emptiness.

Neil was detained and questioned and, when the police were satisfied, they offered us a lift to where they had left the scooter. We got out of the police car to discover that we were back at the forest we had just left. Hell!

It was getting late and there was nowhere to go except back into the forest. We searched deep into the woods, looking for a place to sleep. We shared scraps of food and, because these were really sad moments for two nice people in abominable circumstances, a little conversation began to trickle slowly through. We made a sort of bed in the wet ferns, with only our clothes to sleep in. The sodden ground was our bed, badgers' barking our lullabies, and although Neil put his arm round me in the night, I felt quite abandoned.

By dawn, we were two shivering heaps upon the brown earth. As I began to stir, I wondered if it had all been a nightmare, but, suspecting it was not, I slowly lifted the lid of one eye, and as it took in the wet grass, the wet trees and the bundle huddled beside me, my heart sank. Neil's back was to me, symbolic of his turning away. We kept up a brave front, and returned home.

It was the merry month of May!

CHAPTER 9

The month of June dawned with clear skies and welcome, fragrant winds. I had been given a transfer back home to Falkirk, and Valerie and her parents, by coincidence, had come to live here when her father was given a headmaster's posting and we found ourselves in the same school, a piece of rare good fortune. Valerie taught in the classroom next door to mine in the Annexe of Bainsford Primary School.

On that fine June morning, I was about to leave for school when a rattle at the door indicated the arrival of the postman. On the carpet lay a letter in the small, black unmistakable hand-writing of Neil. Two greedy hands tore it open without delay, and greedy eyes devoured.

Each small, black word fell like a thunderbolt upon my unhappy head. My silent cry rang out across the world. Neil had ended our relationship. It was all over. My body trembled under the weight of a crushing despair which I could not discipline with a clear and obedient thinking. Every little tendril of an eager and loving heart was torn from its place of worship in one decisive stroke.

Out of the valley of Rasselas went the sun; love, the divine gift, the moving spirit of the universe, was gone. Gone were the exhilarating airs I'd breathed; gone the red and purple hues of landscape; gone the pilgrim journey on uncharted seas. Gone, all gone! I bowed my head as my life seemed to pass away from me.

He wrote, 'I know it cannot console you to know that no other girl will suffer on my account as you have; I hope never to encourage another towards whom my feelings are uncertain.'

And he ended his letter thus: 'If I were to suffer similarly, I feel I should be helped by a greater detachment than you are able to command and the possibility of transmuting the most painful experiences into impersonal Art.'

So there I was, a shrinking, suffering thing, 'pitched past pitch of grief' in the first crisis of my young life and none would ever be quite like it again.

'Oh Valerie, help me! Help!'

But Valerie was far away and could not help. She'd gone off to the school camp.

Some inexplicable animal instinct drove me to get away from the hell that threatened me. Blindly I followed its lead. I saw the door knob. I knew I must turn it. Then I would be in the street and if I followed the street, I would come to the school. I knew I must move and keep moving, but I knew not to think. Approaching school one thought dominated my mind. I whispered to myself: *This morning must be like every other. The children have nothing to do with my grief. All must be as it has always been.*

I walked into the building annexed to the school and along a narrow corridor which would lead me to my room – in a rigid manner, zombie-like – and there at her post sat Mrs Esplan, the school cleaner.

She was an elderly woman with the blackest eyes I had ever seen, and long, black hair which unusually hung in waves over her shoulders. But it was her smile that drew me, a smile that sat like Majesty on a throne. Struggling with emotion, and trying to hold it back, I saw the smile, sumptuous and life-giving. The agony burst from me. I held out my hands and she took them in hers. Briefly I told her what had happened, then I had one request of her.

'Mrs Esplan, can you help me into the classroom?'

Without fuss or frown, she took my arm.

'I want to be at my desk for the children coming in.' Gently she ushered me into the room.

The pupils came in; I lifted my head and the day began. I only remember a great sense of wonder as I, with utter fascination, watched my hand write across the blackboard, but what I wrote I never knew.

I saw her watch me through the glass door; she kept her steady eye on me when she should have gone home, and each kindly stare and smile held me together. I felt the tenderness that Thomas de Quincey expressed when he recalled 'the noble-minded Ann', the street walker, who ministered to his needs, when all the world stood aloof from him. He wrote: 'Some feelings, though not deeper or more compassionate than others, are more tender, and often when I walk at this time in Oxford Street, by dreary lamplight, I shed tears.'

She showed an earnestness in helping me which never wavered, patience that was never exhausted and a spirit of warmth which was more than anything I could ever repay or hope to deserve.

The waking time was the hellish time when, stirring from sleep, thoughts would come, gathering along the horizon of my mind, and I proposed not to face them. As I dressed, I trembled in a race to get out of the house before a single thought would strike.

'Oh Valerie, it was like dying,' I told her when she came back. 'I rushed up to school. Mrs Esplan was good to me.

'Did you not stay off?'

'How could I? I had to run.'

'How did you do in school?' she asked.

'I don't know how I did. I worked.'

'What did your mother say?'

'She doesn't know. I've never told her much. I didn't want to hurt her.'

'But she's met Neil.'

'Yes, but I've never told her what I really feel about him. I always suspected something awful like this would happen.'

'But she's bound to see how unhappy you are.'

'I don't propose to let her see. I've left a note to tell her that I've gone to stay at grandpa's because he's lonely and needs company for a little while.'

'It's a shame.'

'Mamma suspects I'm unhappy, but she would never say anything in case it would make me worse. She's like that. She just stands by to help. She's always there like a great protector. Oh, I'd hate to hurt her, Valerie. That's what makes me panic. I don't want to hurt her.'

Raising her arms in a gesture of defeat Valerie said, 'Oh Eilidh, I don't know what to say.'

'I'll have to run. I think I'm panicking. I'll tell you more later. I'll see you . . .'

'No! Don't go,' she said, taking my arm and settling me down. 'Just take your time. I'll stay with you. Keep talking, but talk more slowly.'

'I've thought of something, Valerie . . . I have a plan . . .'

'Right, now try to calm down and tell me your plan, and you might begin to feel better,' she suggested.

I sat for some moments trying to collect myself.

'Something else happened, Valerie,' I said. 'I'll tell you about that first, because it was the most important thing that ever happened in my life.' Valerie's eyes never left my face. 'He wrote to me exactly a week later. He said he was sorry for me and that I could write to him again if I wanted to, just as I would write to an acquaintance. Valerie, my breath came back to me. I was "recalled to life." The feeling of relief far outstripped all other feelings I've ever had in my entire life.'

'Oh, Eilidh.'

'He can never know my gratitude.'

'Eilidh, you'll get over this, you'll see,' she said, her voice softening.

'Maybe.'

'So did you say you had a plan?'

'Yes.'

'What do you propose to do?'

'Well,' I explained, 'It's almost the summer holidays. I'll go away when the holidays begin. No one will see me or know the pain I'm feeling. I'll set off for the Highlands and just start walking.'

'Where to?'

'I don't know.'

'You don't know? What do you mean "you don't know"?'

'I don't know.'

'But you'll *need* to know.'

'No. That's the point. I'll just keep walking and see what happens. Nothing will be planned. I won't even know where I'm going to sleep at night.'

'But that's terrible.'

'I know it's terrible. I'll be frightened and lonely. My nerves will probably get frayed. It'll help me forget him.'

'You mean, one misery will block out another?'

'Yes.'

'Are you sure?'

'No, I'm not at all sure.'

'I wouldn't do that if I were you Eilidh. I don't think it would be good for you.'

'I know, but I can't think of anything else. I'm too shocked. I know I'm clutching at straws but it seems better to clutch at a straw than sink into a black hole.'

'Are you sure you wouldn't rather stay at home?'

'God, no! If everyone sees how unhappy I am it'll make things worse. I'm sorry, Val, but I must try to make it work; it's fight or fall.'

Valerie left for the Continent that summer and I set off, pack on back, to test my theory. On the day I set off, I was lucky to get a lift to Dingwall on an old gas lorry, and when I arrived there about five o'clock, I took my bearings for the west and set off on my trek, on that quiet road which would eventually take me to the Highlands. After I'd covered about fifteen miles, festoons of grey cloud in the distance darkening the hills reminded me that I must soon find a place to sleep for the night. It was almost ten o'clock.

Just then, as all the creatures of the night were snuggling down to sleep in nests of warmth, I passed a little village inn, and the rosy glow spreading outwards towards me made me hesitate, and my footsteps drew up close. I peered in. For a moment I almost succumbed, and it was very hard for me to push on.

There was just enough light left for me to discern a broad river with massive clumps of bracken flanking either side. Knowing of the midges, I moved on. Just as darkness was about to fall, I reached the forest, bounded by a high deer fence. When at last I found the padlocked gate, I opened it and went in.

The last of a cloud's silvery lining gave me light enough to discern the ghostly outline of trees, but wishing to be on the edge of the forest I quickly found a stable platform where a tree had spread her roots on top of a bed of sodden leaves. I spread out my inadequate sleeping bag, thin as it was, drew a frugal piece of cheese from my pack but, as the midges gathered, eating became impossible. Tense, taut and cold, I listened to every sound of the forest, a forest which would not go to sleep, my only comfort an occasional glimpse of the moon.

Midnight came and darkness finally enclosed the forest and its haunts. However, sometime later, I heard in the distance the moan of a car, a moan which came closer and finally stopped at the forest. Strange, I thought. Listening, I heard the car door bang, followed by the rattle of the padlock on the gate. Immobilised, like the hunted animal, I eventually managed to lift my head.

I heard the voices of men which grew louder and came in my direction. I lay under a bank of ferns. These men were about to stumble upon me. I closed my eyes. *'Any minute now,'* I thought. *'I'll beg them to have pity on me. I'll explain. They'll understand, and they'll take me away from this awful place.'*

But the sounds lessened and the voices trailed away. After that, I think I slept in shock until a shot rang out in the woods. *Hunters.* I waited in the hope they would return and, when they finally did and passed again, the forest gate was closed and I heard the car drive away. But I panicked shortly afterwards when I realised that they might have padlocked the gate, and if so I would be trapped in an unendurable hell, for I was claustrophobic. I jumped up in fear and groped my way in the darkness, crawling and stumbling over bracken and gnarled roots, but found the gate was not locked and I was safe. The ordeal over, I fumbled my way back and into the sleeping bag and, at last, fell asleep.

In the night, the biggest brown rat I had ever seen, a rat with coarsened hair, came through the forest, sniffed around me and sank its teeth deep into the soft flesh of my leg. I felt no pain but saw the gruesome spectacle of the teeth emerging from the torn flesh and the thick gush of blood. For this very purpose, I had brought a big, kitchen knife and now I plunged it into the exposed side of the rat and, lifting the bleeding carcase, tossed it to one side.

As soon as that gory episode was over, the enemy of the forest that I had really feared, a heavy-bodied muscular animal, now came tugging at my bag. I mustered all my strength to deal with this powerful foe, but my strength ebbed away in proportion as I gathered it.

These were two of three nightmares that made my stay in the forest a harrowing one and mercifully awoke me at 4 a.m. Ironically, the first thought that came to me as I woke was of Neil, whose memory I'd hoped to banish, and that was the worst cut of all.

I wanted to leave the forest, but at that time of morning, where could I go? So I lay for three more hours.

I left the forest as in a fantasy of nightmare. I walked along the empty road on a grey early morning wondering how I could have arrived at such a point of inner desolation. Lord Byron said. 'The great object of life is sensation; to feel that we exist even through pain.'

But I felt so much pain it made me wonder if indeed I did exist. 'Is this really happening to me?' I asked myself. Disbelieving I could feel such unhappiness, a puddle of water at the roadside made me feel I should test its reality. I dipped my toe in and was quite shocked when I saw a ripple in the water. So it was real.

Shortly afterwards, a big lorry came trundling along the road and stopped ahead of me. I knew the driver was about to offer me a lift, and on that morning of my life I was drawn like a magnet to the little human company it offered. One heave of a hairy arm and I found myself in the cabin. Two heavily tattooed arms swung the lorry into the road, and the driver, in tartan shirt and ponytail, drove off. After the ghosts of the night, his was a welcome, substantial presence.

'You're early on the road,' he said, obviously expecting an explanation.

'That's because I was up early,' I said, ingenuously.

'You can say that again! I thought I was the only one on the road this morning. Where did you come from?'

I decided to tell the truth.

'I slept in the forest.'

He turned from his driving and looked at me, his eyes questioning. He returned his gaze to the road again, but almost immediately turned and looked at me again, as if trying to decide whether to believe me or not.

'But there are wild cats in these forests,' he said. 'Weren't you frightened?'

'Yes, I was.'

'What was it like?'

'I'll never do it again.'

'You're lucky you didn't get a sharp set of teeth in your arse.'

'Oh, but I did,' I said, 'in my dreams.'

He seemed to contemplate what I said and then turned to glance again at me as if trying to match what I said with the person he was looking at.

'I just wanted to see what it was like,' I told him now, wishing to spare him the truth. 'I am a terrible coward really.'

'Well, I admire you for doing that,' he said, then, changing the subject, asked me where I was heading.

'I'm going north and west. I'm just walking and I'd be happy to get a lift as far as Gairloch, if you're going that way.'

'Sure, I'll be passing that way so I'll drop you off there.'

However, he wanted to stop for breakfast and said he would share it with me. We pulled in to the roadside. 'You're a schoolteacher, aren't you?'

'And you're a mind-reader, aren't you?' I replied, and we both laughed.

His breakfast was a big tin of cakes.

'This is what my wife gives me for breakfast, but I'll never know why. She fills this tin with cakes, scones and sponges . . . come on, have some.' I ate his cake, shared his strange breakfast, and devoured his kindness.

Passing through Kinlochewe near Loch Maree, the road to Craig, where Neil was, branched off. I gazed into the distant solitudes of mist, where he was, whose being was once all my most precious world.

The driver gazed too. 'What a hellish place that must be,' he said. 'It's always covered in mist. I'd hate to spend a holiday there.' For myself, I couldn't speak.

I thanked him when he dropped me off a Gairloch and he went happily on his way.

I sauntered, idled and wandered and managed to pass the whole long day, and when evening came I entered the hostel and soon moved into the spacious and tidy kitchen where a few people were preparing meals. Now and again I caught snippets of conversation. Suddenly, from the various mumblings around me I picked up the word 'Craig'. It was like a bolt of electricity!

It came from the mutterings of the bigger of two men who now moved between the cooker and the lockers. The eye of the hunter fixed on its target. With calculating steps I walked from locker to cooker, closing in on my prey. Now he was stirring a stew on the stove. With skilful manoeuvre I found myself also stirring a stew on the stove. I tried to be unobtrusive but, when he moved to the table to eat, I found myself sitting opposite him. He was a big, red-faced sunburnt man in a short-sleeved shirt, open at the neck and he had the appearance of having walked a long way. I moved in for the kill!

'Did I hear you say you'd been to Craig?'

He looked up, finished chewing and replied. 'Yes, that's right.' I knew not to irritate a hungry man when he was eating. I tried to be patient. Pretending a calm I did not feel, I continued, 'And what did you think of it?'

'I liked it,' he answered, continuing to tuck in. 'It was my first visit.'

Deceitfully, I said, 'I was thinking of going' and I pretended, deceitfully again, to be interested in my food. 'What's it like?'

He didn't seem to mind answering my questions so long as I gave him time in between mouthfuls.

'Oh, it's very small and I suppose you could say it was a bit primitive, but I like it that way.' At that moment I didn't care what he liked!

Then I held my breath, and though more attention was given to his food than to my questioning, I asked, 'and what did you think of the warden?'

He stopped for a moment, looked up with a concentrated look, and I hung on every word that followed.

'Come to think of it, he was a strange sort of lad.'

'What do you mean "strange"?'

'Well . . . hmm . . . it's hard to say exactly . . . sort of satisfied with himself, if you know what I mean.'

'No not really. What do you mean "satisfied with himself?"' I was beginning to attract curious stares.

'Well, what I meant was that it seemed to me he was the sort of chap who could put up with a lot of his own company.'

The inquisition continued.

'Was he nice to everyone?'

'Well, come to think of it, he was quite strict. He had quite a row with one lad.'

'Really?'

'Yes. He'd been trying to light a paraffin lamp and the flames shot up. The warden was angry and told him he should never have attempted such a thing without an understanding of paraffin lamps. In fact, come to think of it, the chap was a friend of his brother.'

The more facts I got the calmer I became, and the more politely I was able to treat him, and although every word I spoke with reference to Neil was a stitch in a wound that tightened, it meant the wound was healing.

After the inquisition, I had a good picture of life at Craig, how Neil was passing the time, that he'd bought a new pair of wellingtons and that he had with him at Craig the complete works of Shakespeare.

All these facts gave me something to mull over for the next few days as I walked many long hard miles, and eventually the time came once more for me to turn my footsteps towards home. I was then able to contemplate what had hindered and what had helped recovery. The discomforts and wretchedness I had endured had weakened and oppressed me further, but on the occasions I'd spoken to others, I had been helped.

I had begun my fight back. I had made a start.

CHAPTER 10

It was now that fate decreed that others would take over my destiny. My plight had not been lost upon my family, and now they would intervene to dispense kindness, each feeding me spoonfuls of her particular brand of medicine.

My sister, just married, and her husband Michael, invited me to holiday with them on the Isle of Raasay, which I had missed visiting previously. It was an offer of kindness which I could not reject, though I felt it wrong for me; but with quiet submission, I accepted.

Raasay is a quiet island, lonely and beautiful. Michael chose a bleak and isolated spot on the rocky and remote eastern corner of the island, at a point where the land jutted out to sea. It was the beauty seen through the eye of the geologist that attended the chosen spot. The mountainous outcrops of rock above, behind and around us belonged to a primeval time, and seemed alien in their form, texture and colouring. Trees were gnarled and moribund. No animal grazed there, nor was there sound of bird or bee. Only mites cringed in the mosses underfoot.

The one ubiquitous sound was that made by the sea. I think it was the angle of the bay and the vertically rising rocks around that caused a sonorous echoing around us night and day, like the valedictory tolling of bells. It was my inner dejection that melancholy fed upon and breathed an alien atmosphere over a scene of innocent beauty. It did not help me to gaze across to the peninsula opposite to know that Neil was there locked within its enchanting mists and mountains. Nothing alleviated the depression I felt, and I recall how often I had to clench my fists and grind my teeth to keep from screaming out. Crushed more and more into myself it seemed 'a desert of eternity'.

However, a measure of relief returned when that stay came to an end and a little more time had passed.

But now mamma was ready with her spoonfuls of kindness. She decided to go to the Highlands for a holiday and invited me to go with her. Once more I went into an environment which was alien to my feelings at that time. But she was a stupendous companion, none better. She knew not to mention Neil; she knew not to pry; she knew not to stare with curiosity. In her conversation, she was gentle, witty and intelligent, and never bored me. She asked nothing of companionship, but accepted the best I could offer, and when I languished in conversation, she stepped in with her own enthusiasm and amply supplied all that I lacked.

And those days too, came to an end.

'The Tree of Life was never quiet,' said the poet Housman, and so it was with mine.

When Neil said I could write to him as I would to an acquaintance, because he felt sorry for me, I clung with the tenacity of a terrier to that life-belt thrown to me. It meant that my life did not break like a bough in the wind, but allowed the possibility of bending, thus easing my way gently back from the elated heights to the prosaic valley, where I would once again plough the humdrum furrow. I remembered what Robert Louis Stevenson said: 'The great thing in life is not to succeed but to continue to fail in good spirits,' and though I hadn't failed in 'good spirits' then, at least, I was coping, and my plan to some extent was working, in as much as I'd had my adventures and journeyings, and time had passed.

I'd used the facility Neil had offered. I'd given him a brief account of my summer wanderings, told him that I'd passed quite close to his hostel and described my encounter with the man at Gairloch, that is to say the cross-examination of James Sharpe of Bathgate, but I gave no hint of how I'd really lived, and now my correspondence was dwindling to a close.

But my summer had been a preparation for leaving and not for continuing a dangerous liaison or swimming again in tempestuous seas. But postcards and letters from him far outnumbered anything I sent to him.

Besides, by the end of summer I was frail, and anything I sent was circumspect and sweated first with careful thought and my correspondence tailed off rapidly. I impersonally sent him a piece of music by Prokofiev and Neil, impersonally, sent me a description of a climb of Liahthach, and then I slowly starved the relationship, so that it would eventually cease to be.

But he wrote and continued to write, which made me burn with a fear that the relationship might recover. In the deep recesses of my heart, of course my love for him burned with a fire that nothing could ever quench, but in this dangerous situation, I took a new initiative. I wrote and told him I was well, recovered from low spirits, reasonably content and happy, and he could now take his absence from me without anxiety. I made it clear that it would be a kindness if he would now maintain a silence, a kindness, I said, I was sure he would wish me to have.

After I'd sent the letter I felt quite depressed, for it had not been an easy decision.

Schooldays took over once more. I wrote nothing.

Six weeks passed. He wrote nothing. By the seventh week, I wondered how much longer I could keep it up, but I did. But Neil was first to succumb. He wrote in the seventh week complaining of 'suffering under a blanket of silence'.

Then he wrote asking if we might meet again. I wondered at him. He had made it clear that there was no future together for us, and yet he continued to write which made me wonder at this perversity. I wrote and asked him why he wanted to see me again.

'Why did I want to see you again?' he asked. 'Why not? Don't you think I often want to hold you again, to console and be consoled? Paper and words don't express the entire personality. Just to be with you, with all of you again . . . there was no mystery, why should there be? You assure me I'll forget you. I could never forget you, though you died tomorrow and no external reminder of you ever reached my senses again.'

This pushed my emotions, which had been trying for some time to settle, to an uncanny intensity, and they burned with a primitive energy and every letter I received bore the mark of my most careful scrutiny. I searched unremittingly for some clue as to his feelings, for mine were, by then, finely-tuned, taut and super-sensitive. It began to cause little threadbare fissures in the rock of my stability, weakened as it already had become.

As time passed, the old scenario returned; I found myself waiting for the postman, with all the attendant expectations.

How many have waited as I waited. How many watched as I watched? From my window every morning, I knew each figure that passed, though my attention was reserved for only one, whose shadow I recognised even before his full form came into view. I still recall the atmosphere of these dry, autumn mornings, how clear and still they were. I knew every late rose in the garden, the angle of each pretty head; not a grass blew but I knew of it, not a leaf turned in the wind, but I saw it. And then I caught his shadow and I held my breath, and when he walked on past the gate he left me stunned and empty.

Brontë immortalised that feeling of receiving a letter when she wrote: 'It felt not flimsy but firm. I went to my bureau and opened a drawer and unlocked a box. I took one more look, folded the treasure, held it to my lips and committed it to the box, shut up the box and drawer and returned to class, feeling as if fairy-tales were true. Strange, sweet insanity and this letter, I had not yet read and did not know the number of its lines.'

84

I grew nervous and perplexed and, since I was becoming thin and pale, I returned once more to my grandpa's, for I did not want my parents to witness my suffering. Besides, my grandpa was in need of company though one must wonder what quality of companionship I could have given. My parents believed that my involvement with Neil was over but could see I was uncommunicative and that something was still wrong, but they did not wish to intrude a presence they knew would be unwelcome. I was, however, to discover that my room was being painted, papered and generally refurbished in a household where money was in short supply, so it seemed they were trying even harder to make my life more physically comfortable or perhaps they felt they had not provided well enough for me.

The knowledge that they suffered too, was a heartbreak that would take a heavy toll, for no king was ever loved by his subjects as my parents were by me.

I had a choice . . . either to return home to the love of my parents, find health and the return of happiness and leave Neil forever . . . or not.

As the autumn winds trailed the clouds through the skies, I wished they could have trailed away the weariness of my terribly unhappy existence then.

Not long afterwards, on a morning in late November, I went plodding up to school and, turning a corner, I met a neighbour who called to me 'Did you see the young man who was looking for you?'

'Looking for me?'

'Yes.'

'A young man?'

'Yes. Said he'd come from Cambridge.'

'Neil!' I gasped.

I ran. I reached the playground. I saw Mrs Esplan.

'It's Neil.' I called. 'Neil's come.'

I ran on, dizzy with joy. I saw Valerie approaching. 'Valerie. Neil's come.' I raced towards her.

'I know,' she said, coolly.

'Do you know where he is?'

'In the Annexe.'

'Did he look well?'

'I thought he was a tramp.' was her cold response.

'Oh, I'm so happy, Val,' I called, and raced on.

Then I saw him, dressed as usual in his ex-army clothes, warm boots and scarf, young and flushed with excitement. So what, if he wasn't the best-dressed young man in town? It didn't matter a tinker's curse to me!

I hurried the children into the classroom, while Mrs Esplan fetched him a seat and settled him comfortably. At break, I took him a mug of hot tea for he looked cold. But I had to get on with my work and from time to time I looked out and gave him a wave. I took him to grandpa's for lunch and in the afternoon I made use of him in the classroom encouraging him to work with the children. He set them tasks and puzzles, and told them a story and offered a book prize to the pupil who could provide the best ending and, later, after buying and reading through several, chose and sent the prize.

While his money lasted, he told me, he had travelled by train and then he took the bus. From his pocket he pulled a handful of loose change, and notes. 'I hope I shall have enough to get me home again,' he said.

'You're quite foolish, Neil, to travel so far on so little.' I did not offer him money for I knew from experience he would not have accepted. "I'd rather sleep rough," he'd told me at that time.

'What have you done with the scooter?'

'Well, I left it in a side-road near my lodgings and someone must have come along and took pity on the superfluous parts with which the scooter was burdened, you understand, and considerably relieved it of some of them, including the spare wheel.'

'Yes,' I said, 'There's a lot of that relief going about,' and I smiled.

'Yes, and the folly of trustfulness still not proved to me, I left the spare petrol can while I pushed the scooter home, and when I returned, by a consequence as natural as it was unforeseen, the petrol can had disappeared.'

'So, you've been freed, you might say, of a few more material encumbrances.'

'You might say that, yes.'

Later that evening, after Neil had washed and refreshed himself, I introduced him to my grandpa and left the two of them while I lit a coal fire in the bedroom.

And that night we sat cosy and alone, and talked.

The question at the back of my mind was why he had come at all, and since I knew he'd come via Edinburgh, I wondered if he'd had some business there.

'I know you've always wanted to see Edinburgh, Neil, and I was wondering if that's why you've come all the way from Cambridge.'

'Goodness no'' he said, quite taken aback. 'You don't think I would travel in the middle of winter and spend all that money just to see Edinburgh?' he asked, and I felt my tension melt away. 'Anyway, I might have a new address soon and won't have so far to travel.'

'How's that, Neil?' And so I got his latest list of complaints, which I found quite amusing, in fact almost anything he ever told me I found interesting.

86

'I'm fed up with my present landlord.'

'Tell me.'

'I'm fed up with his unobtrusive snooping. I'm beginning to feel like an interloper there. He's continually coming in and out of the kitchen on some pretext or other, but really to see what I'm doing.'

'Like a spy?'

'Yes, he takes every opportunity for suggestions. For example, which towel I'm to use, or how far to leave the door open, that sort of thing. It's the air of veiled resentment, as if I were deliberately taking advantage every time his back was turned.'

'I suppose you wouldn't mind if he were frank.'

'No, I wouldn't mind in the least. And what's more, they're overcharging me for my breakfast and all I get is a bowl of cornflakes and coffee.'

'You're being exploited too?' I could see he was quite indignant.

'Yes, I think I've told you about him and his wife before.'

'Is it the Polish couple?' I asked.

'Yes, but I won't be with them for much longer.'

'And what else have they been getting up to?'

'Well, they asked me if I would pay for my breakfasts in advance, and I agreed. Last Saturday I went to a concert and was so late getting back that I didn't want to disturb them, and Saturday night is when I pay them. Now, they go to Mass every Sunday and I didn't offer it on Sunday in case their religious principles might be offended.'

'Oh Neil,' I interrupted, 'how could you be so naïve. Greedy people have few such principles. But go on . . .'

'Well, I think you're right. He came in on Sunday, and I'd just rearranged the furniture – no doubt a double blasphemy against the God-given order of things in his eyes – and asked for the money. I explained the reason for my delay, and he told me there was nothing in his religion about not taking money on a Sunday. Well, how infinitely superior of it, I thought. He told me he had no principles of that kind. *Well, how useful*, I thought. When I offered him a cheque he refused it and so I had to pay him in all the cash I had. You see, I'd planned to come up and see you, and I thought I wasn't going to manage.'

The fire seemed suddenly to grow the brighter in these moments.

He could have saved himself the expense and the unpleasantness of greedy landlords if he had found a teaching post near home and, wondering about this, I put this point to him.

'Why didn't I teach at home?' he said. 'Because I didn't want to be defeated near home, that's why. If I was to fail – and I anticipated failure because I had a certain foreknowledge that I wouldn't fulfil myself or satisfy my own standard and ideals of what teaching should be – then I preferred to fail in comparative obscurity, at a distance that softened and blurred the contours of defeat, not with every detail lit up as if by a spotlight and all the unheroic drama acted out in the sight and hearing of my friends and many local acquaintances.'

It sounded so typical of Neil to expect defeat, and it was this that troubled me so much. Where had such a pessimistic attitude come from? What bred it?

'Neil,' I said, snuggling up to him at the fireside, 'you've got it in you to be a great teacher some day, whether you anticipate failure or not. You are imagining a time that may never come to be.'

He put his arm round me and ran his fingers through my hair. 'My mother often says the worst is all behind me.'

I wondered. It sounded like the wishful thinking of a loving mother for her son.

As it was growing late and he had the daunting journey back next morning I told him he would be unfit for work if he did not get to bed.

'No Eilidh, it doesn't work that way. I don't sleep well at night.'

'But it's not good for you to get so little sleep.'

He moved closer to me. 'You see, my brain won't slow down. And then I have dreams. My dreams are so real, Eilidh, that I can't distinguish between them and reality. But they are interesting and I write about them in detail.'

'But the whole essence of dreaming is that you experience them, but don't remember them afterwards.'

'But my dreams are so clear,' he persisted. 'Often in my dreams is the motif of this person that I will meet some day and at some time in the future. I seem to know this person, but not the name, and, do you know, my dreams have a beginning, a middle and an end. That's why I can talk about them and write about them.'

All this new information jolted me.

'But even nightmares are different,' he said. 'Once every few months I have horrible nightmares and I have to force myself awake.'

I found these insights quite harrowing; I had no answer to them nor knew of any remedy.

'Why don't you listen to music before you go to sleep, or even read a book? Lots of people find that helpful.'

'No, I've tried that. It doesn't calm me down. It has the opposite effect. It makes me worse; it stimulates my mind.'

'What about painting?'

'No, painting has the same effect.'

I could think of nothing else.

'You would expect the mind to slow down at night, wouldn't you?' he continued.

'I suppose it should,' I replied.

'Well, mine becomes alive. It goes faster and faster.'

His voice had become soft now as if telling his deepest secrets, and to think I believed I knew already all his sad secrets. Manifestly I hadn't.

'Do you know something, Eilidh?' he whispered close to my ear, 'I can be immersed in a book of philosophy, while listening to music in the background, and as if that wasn't enough, I could tell you how many times the clock had ticked. And even that is not enough. My mind is still not satisfied. You can't imagine the agony that is for me.'

'I'm so sorry Neil,' I said, 'But I've heard that a possible chemical imbalance in the brain could cause these sorts of problems, and that the imbalance can be treated medically.'

'I don't want to give in to any medicine,' he said. 'I'm afraid of what might happen if I were given the wrong drugs.'

He sat looking at me for a long time before he said sorrowfully. 'I don't want to make you unhappy, Eilidh.'

I finally left him to make some supper. I had resolved none of his problems and none of my own.

Before we finally went to bed he wanted to tell me about a couple of childhood memories which seemed to have plagued him.

'Some things happened in my childhood that I've never been able to forget. I once had a neurotic science teacher, for example, who lost his temper with me on one occasion. He made me stand on a chair in front of the class, and he shouted and made fun of me.' I realised the cruel hurt this would have caused a sensitive child.

He went on, 'It was a dreadful childhood experience for me. I tried to save myself by concentrating very hard and pretending this was happening to the boy behind me. It was like turning myself to a stone.' I listened with bowed head. 'It was a bad experience for me because, ever since, I've had a habit of turning myself to stone whenever I'm criticised. I tend therefore not to benefit from genuinely given criticism.'

'That's rather extreme armour to wear, but I understand.'

Before we turned in for the night he told me, 'Eilidh, I still don't know where I'm going. I'm mixed up as I always am. It's as if I need a burden of conscience. All my life has been like this.'

We pulled the bedclothes down from the bed, wrapped them round us and fell asleep in each other's arms.

'Oh, what a knot of tension has gone,' he whispered.

After he left next morning. I was more uptight than usual when I realised I had solved nothing. This doomed relationship was dragging relentlessly on.

Somewhere I read that, by regarding an object under all its forms, turning it over, piercing through it, we at last deform it and give it a character which, in reality, it does not possess. I began such a scrupulous examination of Neil's letters to discover some clue as to why he continued to write, and inevitably there would be distortions.

One day a letter came from Neil, and as I looked hard at the envelope, I saw that my name had been superimposed upon another and the word 'Miss' was clearly discernible. Now I had always known that Neil prepared the cream of foreign students for Cambridge, but it had never troubled me at all. Now it was different because, at this inopportune time in my life, a strange and unwelcome visitor intruded. Jealousy was something new and destructive and an accomplished achiever.

I wondered to whom this letter had been addressed and why and what was the attraction, and what was he writing about? I couldn't ask and give myself away, and I couldn't discover the answer; and I could not get rid of the jealousy I felt.

Long afterwards, I discovered it had been addressed to an elderly warden of one of the women's colleges.

This was followed by another letter asking me to give an opinion about a piece of prose. Normally this would have been a boost to my self-esteem. Not any more. I examined the extract, fully praiseworthy, but I found my concentration an unwilling accomplice. Who had written it? One of his students? Then she must be very talented. How he must admire her. I knew I couldn't write like that. However, he had asked for my opinion, so I took up my pen to answer. But my pen refused to write. Deep down I wanted to find a flaw, something to spoil, something to be scathing about. I searched for some criticism, but none would come. Honesty did finally prevail. I wrote and told the truth. Long afterwards, I discovered that it came from the pen of James Joyce!

As daily life became more turbulent and Christmas approached. I sought out Alistair, then studying in Edinburgh. We walked the wide pavements in the winter sunshine and he was a kind companion who did not preach to me, for I felt my soul was past saving . . .

I went home for Christmas but scarcely noticed those around me, all those who loved me most in the world. I didn't much enter into the festivities, nor could I take a tease. *I did the worst to them I loved the most.*

In the months to come, my mind would become a battlefield where heart and head would become locked in combat.

'Doubt is not a pleasant situation but certainty is absurd,' said Voltaire.

I was becoming very confused.

The old year was slipping away with all its little ironies and tragedies, and once more I tried to finalise everything, but I was almost beaten by the conflict. I wrote, 'Do not reply to this letter. You sent me enough home truths in June. Don't blame yourself for my unhappiness, but this is as fair a warning as I can sound. If you have to be cruel to be kind, then please let it be now. I cannot live through another summer like last.'

Then, probably confusingly, I added, 'If you do come again, then how happy I should be, but don't come for any insincere reason.'

Thus the year ended as he sent me this:

'Thank you for all you write. You are much too kind to me. I know how you feel; I can't live for the moment either. I am rather sad and empty right now. I don't remember a holiday less happy or wasted than this one.'

Alistair revived a little life, however, when he invited Valerie and myself to London, where for a spell he had been working among London's poor. Valerie was excited by the prospect of a little sight-seeing, and it presented an opportunity for me to meet up again with my friend Bob and meet his new girlfriend, Sheila.

When Neil heard of this, he asked if he might join us for part of Saturday and we all agreed, though I made it clear that the week-end belonged to Alistair.

But it boded ill for Neil, because he was accepted by the group on sufferance, rather than receiving a full-blown welcome. Valerie was becoming a little alienated from Neil because he still wrote to me; Bob had only spent an evening in Neil's company; and Alistair was not at all happy when Neil was late arriving at our meeting place, Cleopatra's Needle. In fact, the party refused to wait, and we arranged that I would wait for Neil and join the group later at the National Gallery.

After that hesitant start, in the evening we dined at a stylish restaurant, but there was a distinct iciness between Alistair and Neil, who occupied opposite ends of the table; and Alistair, who should have known better had kept trying to block Neil out of the conversation.

But when we left the restaurant, and when no one was looking, I took Neil aside and gave him a big hug.

The remainder of the evening, however, was very pleasant. Alistair went off to visit friends, and Sheila took us back to her flat, where we sat and talked.

Bob got out his guitar and the long, busy day was completed with playing, singing and supper which Sheila made for us, although she did not stay with us, having a piece of artistic work to complete.

The atmosphere late that evening was soft and harmonious, and everyone succumbed to it. Even Valerie, normally a fidget, sat very still and contented, and Neil came ever closer and placed his hand over mine.

That night I lay in my sleeping bag with Neil on my left – for he had asked to stay – and Valerie on my right. When I heard her soft snores I stretched my hand across to where Neil lay, and he instantly grabbed it and tightly held it in his own.

Morning came, and after washing and breakfasting, clattering and chattering we then all dispersed.

But before I left London and, unknown to anyone, I left a little gift of money for Sheila, who had cared for us, fed and entertained us with such kindness.

Soon after my return home she returned the money with a letter, saying that if she ever came to Scotland I could perhaps give her a place to lay her head.

But she continued the letter with a reference to Neil and myself which said, 'As for Neil, I think you are mad to go gadding about after him. He's nice enough, but obviously not in the least interested in being trailed by you. In fact, that would just turn me sick if I were a bloke! Does he even know how you feel about him? Well, it's not my business, but I can't enjoy seeing people making themselves ill over a spirit in the clouds. You can't be serious about going all the way to Cambridge just to see him'

Oh, would some power guide me out of this fearful country was my cry of despair.

It was after four o'clock, but I rushed up to school in the hope that Valerie would still be there, and I found her in the staff-room doing corrections. Anguished, I shook her, and she, seeing me crumbling under despair and with the telling letter in my hand, took me by the arm and rushed me into her classroom. I just sat and stared ahead. She pulled a postcard from her handbag, laid it in front of me, put a pen in my hand and ordered, 'Write!'

I was sitting at a table and in a half trance. I meekly took the pen, and she dictated and I wrote. 'I've made a decision that is final. Valerie and I are going abroad to work. We leave in July.'

I stopped and looked up at Valerie. She towered over me. 'Write!' she thundered. I continued, and wrote to her dictation; 'There will be no turning back from this decision.' Here, once again, I hesitated. Valerie prodded me with a ruler.

'Tell him,' she said, 'that it is very unlikely that you will ever see him again.'

'Oh, Valerie, I can't!'

'Go on!' she barked. 'Tell him this is the end of the affair.' I looked up at her face, dark with hostility, and I wrote. 'Sign it!' she yelled . . . and I did.

'Now,' she said, slowly and solemnly, 'give me your word that you will write no more.'

'I promise.'

'Now go out and post the card. Now!'

Taking the card, I walked slowly to the door, but she stopped me and grabbed it back from me.

'I wouldn't trust you! I'll post it myself!' She rose to go.

'Oh, don't go, Valerie!' I pleaded. 'My conscience is so uneasy!'

'The break has to be made,' and, gathering her things together, she started to leave.

'But just let me wait a bit yet,' I pleaded. 'Let me put it to him more kindly,' I begged.

'It's now or never!' she declared. 'You're going back on your pledge already.'

'Oh, don't be so cruel, Valerie! I'll do anything you ever ask of me if you'll just let me write more kindly.'

'No!' And she was gone.

Thomas Hardy truly said, 'Statesmen think and think, then act. Women act then think and think.'

I became a traitor.

I wrote to Neil!

I told him what Sheila had said in her letter, but he dismissed that as 'high-flown fantasy'.

He said he wanted to explain something to me which he had never told anyone, and which he had committed only to his diary: 'I've always felt acute pain and disconsolateness when I'm part of a group in which I'm a little neglected or ignored. If in a group of three or more, I am particularly interested in one only I deliberately concentrate on, and favour, those to whom I am least attached. This is almost instinctive in me now as to be automatic. Sheila was surely unwise to judge me, as such swift conclusions suggest . . . it's funny and pathetic all at the same time. But, why or why do you place more reliance on your friends' judgements and persuasions than on your own sense and feelings?

'And if you will believe that I was reluctant to come to you at night, then you will believe anything. God, how my acquired English reserve betrays me. Intimacy had to be forfeited because I was in a damn chastity bag!'

But what I'd said about going abroad was, of course, untrue - just a ruse - but Neil believed it and wrote: 'I never feel that any meeting between us will be the last. But if you think I won't miss you when you are abroad, then you're mistaken. You're mad, a fool, however indifferent about people you believe me to be. I *shall* miss you. I shall not forget you. I could not forget you even if I wished to.

'Tell me all the promises I've failed to keep and I'll fulfil them all. What would you like me to do for you, now, before you go?'

Once I had proposed that we might one day share a flat together and now he commented: 'I often think of your proposal to share a flat together, a sort of mock, extended-working honeymoon I think I should have been as little unhappy with you as I should be with anyone. You see, *you* are capable of happiness, whereas *I* am rather capable of *un*happiness, and I feel a guiltiness towards you, because I am depriving you of joy - a joy which could be yours more permanently with someone else - and, by prolonging our relationship I'm injuring your chances of finding that someone else.'

It was the month of May.

CHAPTER 11

Once again the month of June dawned fresh and sweet, exactly one year after Neil ended our relationship.

Pale, starved, weak and exhausted, illness came to bring the struggle to an end.

'Inconsistent soul that man is,' said Sterne, 'languishing under wounds which he has the power to heal, his whole life a contradiction to his knowledge.'

I had a nervous breakdown.

Neil ceased to exist; so, too, did correspondence. I was in the hands of others. Family and friends did everything to help me recover, and many weeks of careful and loving nursing would slowly bring me back to health.

Often, as I lay in bed, my dream was to get back to the mountain fastnesses, to be free once more as I once had been, 'with the wild moment'.

Life progressed much as in a vacuum until, at the end of summer, Valerie suggested that we go to the North-West for a holiday. Adrian, my old friend from 'Acheninver days' wanted to come with us, and she felt the fresh air and company would do us all good.

The back of the car just managed to contain the lanky, sprawling form of Adrian. Everything he did was slow and deliberate; even his laughter came in slow guffaws, with the simultaneous rise and fall of his wide shoulders. His was the best company one could have had, for he was game for any nonsense in which we might indulge, and he was happy doing what we were doing, and to please this young, good-natured boy was a joy for us.

Our holiday was the typical highland carry-on that we were used to . . . eating in the open, washing in the mountain streams, walking, climbing and generally being unsophisticated. We stayed at my old hostel in Achittibuie. I was surprised at how quickly the wildness captured my spirit again.

A new friend we made at this time was an unsuspecting chap - Mike, a chemist from Birmingham - who had arrived alone for a holiday. He was tall, clear-eyed and good-looking, and Valerie lost no time in drawing him into the group.

One sunny afternoon we decided to go shopping to the little village of Lochinver.

'Do you want to come with us?' Valerie asked Mike, but before he could answer, he was dragged into the car and we were speeding along the narrow roads in the summer sun and wind. It was typical of Val's boldness; she could quite suddenly lose the heavy burden of life that seemed to drag her down so often at home.

She suddenly stopped the car at the foot of Stac Polly, a beautiful mountain of one thousand feet, an easy climb.

'Out!'

'What do you mean "out"?' asked Mike, with a hint of a smile.

'Out, because we're going to climb the mountain!'

'But I don't want to climb the mountain,' came the reply, with slight irritation.

'What you want has nothing to do with it!' said the bold girl.

We all got out of the car, including Mike, still protesting.

However, with a smile on his handsome face, he was soon following us up the mountain and, like the rest of us, relished every minute of it, especially the view when we reached the top.

After lingering there for a while I said suddenly, 'Right! I was the slowest up but I'll be the fastest down!' and I slipped my waterproof jacket under my bottom, sat down, and took off. I found myself sliding, bumping and spiralling downwards, and then, looking up into the mists above, saw Valerie and the others come sprawling and sliding downwards on the dry areas of grass and heather after the same fashion.

We left again and Mike offered to take over the driving to give Valerie a rest, and we snaked along the narrow roads, waving to drivers as they passed. However, I noticed soon enough that Mike ignored this courtesy.

'Did you see that, Valerie?' I said.

There was soon an indignant chorus clamouring for his 'resignation'.

Mike, embarrassed at first, soon rose to the occasion.

When the next car passed, Adrian doffed his cap, Valerie threw kisses, I waved and Mike gave a right royal flourish of wrist and exaggerated salute.

'Will that suit you then?' he asked.

'It'll do,' I said.

We were determined to make his stay with us a memorable one.

After shopping in Lochinver we went our separate ways for a while and Mike followed me to a local bar for refreshment. I found the barman unusually unfriendly. When we left, I took Mike to a grassy verge, sat down and surprised him.

'See what I've got,' I said, shaking my sleeve, as two chocolate bars came tumbling out. 'One for you and one for me.'

'You don't mean you stole them?'

'I lifted them when he wasn't looking,' I said. 'I didn't like him. Did you?'

'No. I didn't like him either, but you must realise that you stole that from the owner and not the barman.'

'Well, it's his own fault for employing someone like that,' I said, 'and don't be so serious Mike.' But he ate the chocolate, despite his protestations.

We continued to have a lot of fun with a lot of friends, but our stay was a short one and, though I was happy, I was still an ill person and had to go to bed early each evening.

Before our holiday came to an end Val insisted that we spend a night at Craig. I didn't want to go but made no fuss. Neil was not there, of course, for I did know his whereabouts but, with a touch of defiance, I wrote my name very clearly in the visitors' housebook. I expected that he would see it sometime during the summer.

But summer's end had come and Valerie returned to school. Months would have to pass before I would be fit again.

Quite by accident, while having supper at a friend's house one evening, I idly turned the pages of a holiday brochure with information about Gloucestershire, and since I thought it looked a pretty place and, as it contained the address of the Tourist Information Centre in Cheltenham, I decided to leave home and go there to work and see what the future might hold for me. It was to be the start of a new phase in my life.

I obtained accommodation in a house in Cirencester and had sent my rent in advance. I had given Valerie my address there, but I was a week or ten days late in arriving in England.

Meanwhile an incident of some sadness occurred at home. I had not known that Valerie had grown fond of Mike and had been writing to him, but he must have asked of my whereabouts and had been given my address by Valerie. Just before I left for Cirencester I bumped into Valerie unexpectedly in Falkirk. She was crossing the road and in a hurry.

With a somewhat distressed look on her face, she called out me, 'I had a letter from Mike! He's been in Cirencester looking for you.' She was rushing in the opposite direction. 'He spent the night sleeping in his car.' She rushed on, with a look of anguish on her face, her voice trailing on the wind.

I was flabbergasted. If Mike was interested in me then he was interested in one who could not return that feeling. Poor Valerie. Fate had pulled off a trick. I had never encouraged Mike. He had never been in my mind, for my mind streamed only with one, and one was all that gave life meaning.

I felt a pang of grief that day, and many others since, for that was my last memory of Valerie, because when I returned after my sojourn in England I learned that Val's parents had died and she had gone elsewhere; rumour had it that she married and went off to live in South America. I knew I would miss her far more than she would ever miss me.

Before I left for England, a letter from Neil informed me that he'd seen my name in the housebook at Craig, which caused the comment, 'Why, oh why, couldn't you have hung on? Remorse and woe have been plucking at me. What a dark sister broods over us.'

I had written very little to Neil that summer, but I did tell him that I had been ill, that he was not to write, and that we should never meet again.

But why, I wondered, did I put my new address on a postcard and sent it to him. I would be no better than he, it seemed, at terminating events, but I was still on medication and, according to Neil, I was writing, 'impossible, contradictory and paradoxical pages.'

But I was about to embark on a new life, and was no longer so dependent on Neil's writing as I once had been, and so, sooner or later, I would find the strength to do what everyone had wished me to do for so long.

I arrived on a darkening evening in the town of Cirencester and soon found the house in Tower Street. I liked at once the dignified red brick building, with its elegant trees and neat, trim little garden, near the town square. It was with some confidence that I walked along the path, I was met at the door by a little old lady, who promptly showed me to my room, gave me a key, asked no questions, showed no interest in me, and left. It was the cleanest, smartest and neatest little room it was ever my good fortune to have. I sighed with relief and happiness.

The following day was Sunday, 15 November and I ventured out into this strange new land. A little ceremony was taking place in the town square and, feeling something of an intruder in this new territory, I slipped into the doorway of a shop to steal sly peeps, and soon realised that it was a Commemoration Service for the fallen of the First World War, which rather saddened the day.

The old church nearby, which seemed to have cheated time and defied crumbling, attracted me and I spent some time inside, comforting after the service outside. It was beautifully and profusely ornamented by rude hands that lovingly fashioned it all of eight hundred years before.

From there I moved to an area of parkland, beautiful too, and, as it was late autumn, there was a stillness that settled upon everything, as if time had been forgotten. The contrast between the wild and gloriously mountainous country of home and the tame, still beauty that was here, was a surprise that delighted

98

me. I gazed at the ancient buildings, antique archways and visited the Museum. I wandered in leisurely fashion, feeling a contentment I did not expect to find so soon in my new life.

I could have stayed there forever in that town of antique beauty, surrounded by a rich and verdant countryside, and no one troubled me in the little house, with its quaint highly polished furniture, its brasses and rich brocades. *I will soon heal here*, was my thought.

My acquaintance was short-lived, however, because there was little public transport to take me to the city for work. Shortly afterwards, I had to leave.

I made my way to the main thoroughfare in Cheltenham where there was a busy Tourist Information Centre and I went in. I approached the main desk where a bespectacled lady was in charge of the accommodation register. I gave her my particulars and the accommodation I required and, after having looked me up and down for some time, she handed me a piece of paper saying, 'I've just the place for you. Go to this address,' and she handed me a name and address. The house was Viola Villa which perturbed me a little, because I felt I could not afford to live in a 'villa'. I had not yet found work and I didn't have much money. I would have mentioned my financial situation to the woman behind the desk but I had the impression that if I had said I was poor, she would have "sniffed". Anyway, as I made my way, my steps became less hesitant when I thought of mamma, who at least would be at rest knowing I had such fine accommodation.

At last I came to the end of a little lane, and there stood Viola Villa. I laid down my luggage and stood facing the villa. I fumbled for the little scrap of paper scrutinized it then swallowed hard.

There, in the middle of an unkempt garden wilderness, stood a dilapidated cottage with four small windows, signifying four small rooms, and in the wilderness close by, a small greenhouse, or what had once been but was no more, with broken windows; chipped and broken plant pots were strewn around between tussocks of grass.

I slowly pushed open the old iron gate, the only substantial thing I could see, and moved slowly towards the front door, while the gate creaked to a close.

It felt strange giving a knock on the door of a home where I felt that the owner must have died a long time before, for only ghosts would be around now. The only movement was the stirrings of spiders in the webs that festooned the door. However, after some creaking and crunching, the door began to open inch by inch, and the thin, rigid face of an Englishwoman was painstakingly revealed.

The painful dilapidation of the place did not surprise me, but that there was life beyond that door did!

So there I was, staring at a rather elderly, gaunt and hungry-looking woman, whose grey hair was tied tightly back in a bun, and I could not help wondering what her nature might be and what circumstances in that house would unfold.

She led me into what I supposed was her living-room and sat down for a moment on a hard chair, presumably to have a better look at me, and she told me to sit down. I thought she was going to make me a cup of tea, but clearly that was not her intention.

While she sat stiffly with her hands in a knot on her lap, I glanced around the room, in which there was a pervading smell of cats. It was darkly furnished with an old brown carpet, a decrepit arm-chair in a corner, a sideboard littered with old papers and magazines and a small alarm clock. The small table, placed beside the chair in which I was sitting held an army of miniature knick-knacks and ornaments.

Whether the carpet was threadbare or not, or whether the sideboard bore the marks of age or the alarm clock was at the right time, there was no way of telling, for the light was poor in this room of sombre colours. It was scarcely possible to decipher the form of the old lady herself in her grey clothes and brown apron, for the greys and browns merged into a sort of soup of brown haze and everything reflected the melancholy dullness.

She caught me looking around the room and was about to get up when a big tomcat, also invisible in the haze, jumped into my lap, filled it and hung over, so that I had to lift my arms to accommodate him, and he showed his pleasure by digging his sharp claws into my flesh.

'Watch he doesn't dig his claws into you,' she warned.

'No, it's all right,' said I.

'Come,' she rose, 'and I'll show you to your room.' We vacated the airless and featureless room to go upstairs and, as I followed the progress of her skinny legs and slippered feet, I noticed a fine layer of dust.

She opened a door and I walked into my room.

It might have been a prisoner's cell; small, austere and with army blankets on the bed, a small table, two chairs, a stone jug and ewer for washing and, for warmth, a small six-inch electric bar on the wall and, for cooking, one single small hotplate.

The room I had left in Cirencester with its shining brasses and its highly polished furniture had twinkled like lights on a Christmas tree.

I was so far away in shock that I scarcely heard her say, 'I certainly like the look of you. I've had some bad 'uns in 'ere, nurses and the like.'

I tried to focus on what she was saying. I looked in her direction.

'The last one I 'ad had a boyfriend and 'e used to come at night and throw stones at the window and she would let 'im in, but I soon put a stop to that. I cleared 'er out.' I saw her lined and hungry face and narrowing, spiteful eyes.

She continued. 'Then he came back and rifled my meter. Anyway,' she paused and took a long, hard look at me, 'you don't look that sort.'

Then she left me to unpack.

I was still partially recovering from my breakdown and I could sometimes get a sense of panic. I stood in my little cell for a moment more, breathed deeply, tried to summon some courage, but my need for human company was too great, and I suddenly rushed downstairs, trying to contain my panic.

'Mrs Shiann,' for that was her name, 'do you think I could have a cup of tea?'

'No,' she replied bluntly. 'You can make it in your own room.' After a moment's pause, she took me back up to my room to show me how the system worked. I wondered how there could be anything to explain.

All the electricity was metered, she explained, but unfortunately if she forgot to put money into her meter, downstairs, then my electricity would be cut off too. Also, she told me, I could not have the hotplate and the fire on at the same time. I was so dumbfounded by this bleak prospect that I could hardly speak. We were well into winter and the hotplate, a mere few inches square, took over an hour to heat a pint of water and, while I was waiting to wash, I had to get into bed. But the bed was so cold and the bedding inadequate, I had to have a hot water bottle, so there was a long waiting time before I could get into bed. Cooking was out of the question, and to make a cup of tea required careful planning.

Later that evening when I was waiting for a cup of water to boil, the lights suddenly went out, I sat waiting for something to happen when I heard her footsteps on the stairs. She told me she would put money in the meter and that 'this time' I could come downstairs and get a cup of tea. I sipped the tea very slowly to make it last, and I desperately longed for conversation, whatever would come through those tightly pressed lips which seemed not to have ever known a smile. There was little animation and, indeed, it transpired she was quite depressed for her husband had not long since died, and she told me: 'I just want to put my head in the gas oven.'

Her state of mind explained why she was so pale and thin.

'I hardly ever eat nowadays,' she told me.

'You have no appetite?'

'None. I just drink tea.'

'Are you attending the doctor?' I asked.

'How can 'e help?' she asked abruptly.

'But he could give you something to make you feel better,' I said.

101

'He can't bring my 'usband back,' and then she burst into tears. I felt it was wise to let her cry and she would probably feel better.

'I've told the doctor I can't sleep for a buzzin' in my 'ead, and he says I'll just have to get used to it.'

The two of us sat in the dull little room, I rather stiffly, until her conversation ended, when I returned uneasily to my own room and waited for the dawn of perhaps a happier day.

In the evenings, however, I walked the streets for a long time before returning in the darkness, and sometimes there was no sign of her; only the pervading smell of cats met me, and in some fear of the tom, I hurried to my room.

In those circumstances I wasn't long in getting temporary work in the Savoy Hotel.

She could have survived without my company, but I couldn't have survived without a little of hers so, occasionally, I crept downstairs on some pretext or other.

But I soon found she was made of sterner stuff than she would have had me believe, and I soon found too, that she missed her husband Bert, for all the wrong reasons.

'He used to carry the dustbin out for me. I'm not able to carry it out myself.'

I offered to carry it out for her.

'He used to do the garden,' she complained, 'and look at it now.'

Then there was the bath he used to fill for her.

After having a good weep, her mood would change, her eyes would narrow and her thin body fill with tension. Then, stiffening, she would say, 'All the while my Bert was in hospital not once did anyone knock on my door to see how he was.' I gave her all the sympathy I could.

When she caught me looking round the room for a moment she added, 'That's why the room is such a pig-'ole. I'm too depressed to do any work.'

'But that doesn't really matter,' I said.

She had nothing nice to say of anyone, and she had nothing cheerful to say at any time.

'You know,' she said to me with angry and grudging voice, 'Bert didn't know how to handle money and we often argued about it.'

'Didn't he?'

Then, shaking her head, she told me, 'Do you know the mortgage on this house isn't paid up yet? If I had had my way it would have been paid long ago.' And in a burst of sympathy for herself, she added, 'And here I am still having to worry about it.'

Winter had arrived with a vengeance in Gloucestershire and my whole being was bent on survival in that house.

It took me all the hours of the evening to wash and, one evening, struggling to wash and half-naked on my knees beside the stone basin, it almost became too much for me. I dressed and, with some temerity, descended the stairs and quietly said, 'Mrs Shiann, do you think I could have a jug of hot water to wash?' and I held out the little enamel jug in my hand.

'No,' was the emphatic reply. 'I can't afford to heat water for you.'

Abashed, I returned to my room, and never asked again. But later, I heard the soft foot on the stair.

'Here's a little for tonight. But I can't give you any more.'

The difficulty was compounded by the fact that often the lights would suddenly go out and, plunged into darkness, I'd have to cover myself in a blanket, grope my way downstairs, following the smells of the cat, and fumble for her meter, which she conveniently forgot to keep filled.

She was really very hard on me. I remember my relief when I discovered the Public Baths because she would not allow me to have a bath in her house. After a luxurious bath one night, I returned home, warm and glowing, but she turned quite sour when I told her where I'd been.

'Don't you know "the Blacks" go there?' she squirmed.

'Gosh,' I said to myself, 'nothing I do is right!'

It was very strange too, I thought, that when she went out at night to Bingo, she locked me in. But the intensity of cold that December was, of itself, an experience.

Perhaps the reason I survived was the intense struggle against this austerity. My philosophy was that of the housemouse: find a shelter out of the storm and keep warm and safe 'till spring comes round again.

But I did my best to please her, for on pay-days after I had treated myself in town to a cream cake and big pot of tea, I would return and always brought her a chocolate cake which always seemed worth the effort to see the lips almost reluctantly move into a smile. But I was often angry that she denied me so many simple comforts.

And I did not write to Neil, as I had promised myself, but a letter was forwarded from Cirencester and clearly my silence irked him.

'Since you have not written, I assume you are enjoying a certain secrecy. On this assumption, the more I should enquire, the less you will impart. I will draw a veil over my current activities, therefore, except to tell you that I called on you for the third time, and found you, for the third time, absent. I found myself in the rear of the premises in Cirencester, in a kind of porch. Pushing my way through the brassières, girdles and shifts, with which the entrance was decorated, hung like bunting, as if to flaunt themselves in the faces of promiscuous salesmen, I reached the back kitchen door. I hammered there, determined that, although no one was in, I would release my frustration, by a savage assault on the panelling. I was later approached by a policeman.

But I did not reply to Neil's letter and I told Mrs Shiann nothing about myself and she never asked.

As the weeks passed by, I did notice a slight improvement in her condition. Because I encouraged her to talk, she would invite me down more often for a cup of tea and she slowly imparted little bits of her life that I tried to interest myself in.

She liked to go to Bingo, for there was plenty of mixed company. Her husband Bert, whom she described as 'a man's man', would only take her out to the pub and she didn't care for that. Nor did Bert want children and, she told me, she had to wait fifteen years before her little daughter came along.

'Of course,' she said, 'once his little girl came along, he doted on her and spoiled her.'

Once, she kindled a spark in me when she told me her mother was Irish. Neil's father was an Irishman, and anything in any way associated with Neil was grist to my mill.

'Really,' I said, wide-eyed. 'Tell me Mrs Shiann, what do you think is the Irish temperament?'

'You're asking me about the Irish temperament. I'll tell you,' she said. 'They're mad!' She continued, 'I had a brother, and nothing in the world would get him out of bed in the morning. My mother could do nothing with him. So, one day, she found a solution.'

'What did she do?'

'She set fire to the bed. I'm telling you,' she said peering into my eyes, 'they're mad!'

So, I noticed that the longer I stayed there, the more she seemed to improve. She began to wear a piece of jewellery when she went to Bingo, sometimes she got her hair done and a little more colour came into her cheeks, though not into mine. But I was surviving.

One pleasant surprise came in the form of a totally unexpected letter from Mike, which had been delivered to my Cirencester address and forwarded. I recalled Valerie telling me that he had been searching for me there. He said he was inviting himself across to see me, but if I disputed, he wouldn't argue for, he said, 'The impressions of the pen are much too positive and lasting, and golden princesses are not easy to find.' He continued, with more poetic charm, 'You must set my mind at rest, for every moment that my mind goes into a daydream slumber, I awake with a song that echoes through my mind. Please release my mind from its craving, for it begins, "The Summer time is coming."'

Amusingly, it was the self-same song I sang to Alan on the shores of Tobermory Bay, all that long time before.

Like a miser with his gold, I stored away in my mind the music of his words, but it was sad that Mike should seek me out, for only one person was, and would be, part of the process of my life, its driving force, the mainstay and the purpose.

He hoped, he said, to show me Housman's country sometime in the future because, he said, 'You have awakened in me a thirst for poetry.'

His short visit was a memorable one. He drove a long way for a two-hour visit and I felt sorry for him because I had not the amenities to be any kind of hostess, but I did the best I could in my circumstances but was depending on Mike's good nature to see us through.

He arrived cold and hungry and Mrs Shiann had gone out to Bingo and, though she normally locked the house when she left, making me a prisoner, she had neglected to do so on that evening. I dreaded what he might think of the place, but he made no fuss and sought no explanation.

Just as he took up his knife and fork to eat, poised for a moment, the lights went out. Silence from him. I moved to get a candle, strategically placed when I planned my 'Winter Campaign'.

'Do you have ghosts, for you did not tell me about them?'

'No ghosts, Mike,' I answered, 'else I would have made friends of them long ago.'

I went to the God-forsaken place downstairs and put money in the meter, and when I returned, there was a flickering of the lights, which Mike attributed to a heavy fall of snow,, but by that time he'd offered to take me out to dine properly and we had a civilised meal.

Before he left that night, he returned me to 'Spook Corner', as he had named it, and I was so grateful that he had kept his good humour.

'I'll give your regards to the ghosts,' I called as he waved good-bye, and I missed him when he left.

Christmas had almost arrived. Once more snow had fallen in Gloucestershire. I was sitting alone in the darkness of my room, wrapped in a grey blanket, watching the snow fall into the emptiness outside, and waiting for the chiming of the church clock to disturb the grave-like silence of the hollow evening when

I heard a banging on the door. It couldn't be! Mrs Shiann had long gone to Bingo. The banging came again. There was no mistaking it . . . someone was at the door!

The thought that there might be another human in that icy wilderness, that there was some form of life outwith my cell, and knocking to get in, shot me into action! Like a whirlwind I was downstairs.

Once in the hall, I rushed to the door, pushing coats on the coat-stand aside, falling over empty boxes and knocking over the umbrella stand in frenzied activity to get to the door.

Someone's out there, I thought as I grappled with the heavy fortress door. I didn't ask who was there. It didn't matter. This was a life-enhancing opportunity not to be missed.

'Oh!' I shouted as I pulled at the lock. There was a slight screeching and grinding but it scarcely moved. After a silence from the icefield on the other side of the door, an impeccably polite voice called, 'I'm looking for Miss McKinlay.'

Flustered, I called back, 'Oh, that's me! I'm Miss McKinlay. Oh, the door's locked! She's locked me in.'

A further ominous silence from outside. I realised that further grappling with the door was useless and once again the scrupulously polite voice called, 'Is Miss McKinlay in?'

'Yes, but I'm locked in!' went my call with some exasperation. 'Oh, wait!' I shouted, remembering the back door. 'Wait a minute! There's a back door!' and I rushed through to the kitchen unable to see in the dark and knocking over the cat's saucer of milk, but eventually getting the back door open. I rushed out into deep snow of bleak winter.

Many things crossed my mind during this encounter with the stranger. For example that this visitor involved in such bizarre circumstances must, by now, be deeply embarrassed and, besides, it demeaned me and put me at a great disadvantage in the eyes of the stranger with the distinguished voice, a mystery still to be solved. In other circumstances I might have scurried away like a mouse into some hole, but I so desperately needed another human being to talk to, that I was prepared to accept the humiliation that was now heading my way. I need only have thought of the cold in the house, the dust, the frailty of the furniture . . . cold tea, bread and cheese, if he was lucky!

In the snow, I realised I was in my slippered feet and still clutching the hot water bottle that I was hugging to keep warm. Ploughing my way through snow which came up to my knees, I met my surprised guest half-way.

'My name is David Irons,' said the tall figure in the dark coat. 'A friend of yours, John Reid, asked me to call.'

'Oh!' I gushed. 'How very kind of John. What a surprise this is. Do come in!'

John Reid was a somewhat dignified young man I'd met at Acheninver; a person who wrote occasionally to me, and this friend of his - beside me now in the snow, a solicitor in Cheltenham - was obviously of the ilk whose expectations of me were about to suffer a violent shock.

My heart gave a little flutter as I led him into the house and I realised the smell of cats would soon come drifting to his genteel nostrils. I'd hoped therefore to hurry him up the stairs but Fate decreed that he should linger and get a good whiff of the cat smell. Opening a bag, he took out a pair of slippers. 'I'll have to take off my wellingtons or they'll wet the carpets.'

'Oh, you needn't bother,' I said, realising he might never see a carpet and realising too, in spite of my exultant exterior, that many shocks were lining up for him.

It seemed to my fraying nerves that he took so long to change into his slippers, and I was so much 'on edge' that in a desperate bid to be kind, I thrust the hot water bottle into his arms. 'Oh, keep yourself warm!' I said, but he instantly returned it. 'Oh, no,' he insisted. 'Please, you look very cold.'

I led him upstairs wishing there was some way I could have hidden the dust.

He held out his coat of beautifully tailored cashmere and I folded it with care and laid it aside. I offered him a poor wooden seat wondering what degree of shock this sophisticated young man must already have suffered, and it added to my anxiety to realise there was more cultural trauma waiting in the wings, when, for example, to offer him a cup of tea would require me to perform a near miracle. Most of the cracked cups Mrs Shiann had given me had already disintegrated.

As I did not want John's choice of ladyfriends to be so abysmal in the eyes of David Irons, I lost no time in explaining the circumstances and, without saying much, he nodded as he listened, at least attempting sympathy, though, if not with Mike's amusing asides, at least he was polite. Though humour was out of his reach as a first line of defence, his manners were polished.

Because I had been for so long starved of company my conversation fell in heavy showers around his willing ears.

He had just returned from visiting the art galleries of Florence, he told me! It registered in my mind how cruelly Fate, at one stroke, can transport one from the Uffizi to the grey room with the army blankets, stone jug and basin!

However, as good luck would have it, I'd recently spent some time in the local library, trying to keep warm, and had been reading a little very basic art, just enough to cover up my ignorance and keep the conversation going. I also had an interest in Edgar Allan Poe at that time, and I managed somehow to work that into the conversation. When I revealed a love of music he told me he played the violin, and he promised to bring it next time he came, so he must genuinely have been enjoying himself.

When I bravely offered to make him some tea, he wisely declined saying he would have to leave as the weather was so bad and he had to get to the opposite side of Cheltenham.

I saw him off the premises, told him I'd look forward to his return, but I never saw him again.

Not long after he left, I heard Mrs Shiann return and unlock the heavy storm doors. Joyfully, I rushed downstairs and caught her as she came in the door.

'Oh, Mrs Shiann!' I said excitedly, and taking her hands in mine, 'I've just had the most wonderful evening.'

I drew her into the sitting-room. 'I had a visitor! It was so unexpected.' I sank into a chair, with a sigh of excitement. 'I must tell you all about it! Someone I've never even seen before!' I looked up at her, and my voice caught in my throat. The dark look on her grim face stopped me dead.

'You let a man into my house?' I knew then I'd made a mistake.

I mumbled. 'Hmm, yes.'

'You let a stranger into my house?' Her eyes were cat-like.

'But it's all right . . . a friend sent him . . . he's a solicitor in Cheltenham.'

'What's 'is name?' she thundered.

In my confusion I'd forgotten. 'I don't know.'

She was incensed.

'You don't know!' she growled. 'Where does he live then?' she uttered between clenched teeth.

'I don't know that either,' I answered, and all my excitement died a final death. 'But,' I protested, 'there's nothing to worry about.'

'And how do you know he's a solicitor?'

By then I knew I was trapped because nothing I could say would soften her attitude.

'A lawyer friend of mine sent him,' I answered.

'I don't believe you!'

'He was so well-mannered, and well-spoken.'

'You had no right to let anyone into my house without my permission. Don't you know there are burglars about? He was probably a thief come to size up my house. Now he'll have a good idea where everything is and the position of everything in my house. Have I told you about the footprints in the snow I've seen recently?'

'No.'

'Well, he might even be a murderer. I wouldn't be surprised if he came back again.'

Innocently I blurted out, 'Yes, he said he would come back and see me.'

'Oh no, he won't. If he ever comes back here, I'll turn him away.'

The thought of John's friend returning to a cold rebuff filled me with dread so I wrote to John and explained what had happened and I never saw David Irons again.

And where was Neil and what was he doing? I never knew for I never wrote, ironically even now, when I had so much I could have written about. But I knew, too, that if life could not be endured with him, neither could it be endured without him. I kept to my plan and when he did not write to me, I felt he was at last making an effort to break away. It was for the best, I told myself, but every day that passed was a shade greyer than the one before.

Mamma paid me a visit over Christmas and was so appalled at my accommodation that she said she would not return home until she had found me another place.

Mrs Shiann cried and offered accommodation free if only I would stay. She told mamma that I was the nicest person she had ever had and I had been like a daughter to her, but unfortunately she had not been like a mother to me. But by that time, anyway, I had managed to get a teaching post in the city of Gloucester and so I went there to live, but I promised to return and visit Mrs Shiann, which I did, and we stayed good friends.

My stay in England would now take me to Dinglewell in Hucclecoat, part of Gloucester, to live with Mrs Stone.

Before I left Cheltenham I dropped Neil a card with my new address, reminding him to 'sleep no unquiet slumbers on my account'. and, though I wrote no more, the flickering flame was never quenched.

He wrote no more to me. So, this was a new beginning of the end, and the best I'd achieved so far.

CHAPTER 12

My new landlady, Mrs Stone, was as fat and well-fed as Mrs Shiann had been skinny and gaunt. Hers was a family life of fulfilling domesticity, and the fulsomeness of her warm and generous presence made me feel I was living under a spell.

At the top of the stairs I had an unpretentious little room. When I went downstairs in the morning, my eye alighted on the one piece of furniture, endowed with a special distinction: the little table in the hall, where any mail was placed.

Watching for letters to arrive had become a daily ingredient of my life, where winged hope would rise defiantly from an alien wish that Neil would write, then drop with exhausted desires. I knew too, that that same distinguished table would undergo a careful scrutiny each time I left the house, and again on my return, for try as I might, I could not moult the worn-out skin of hoping to hear from Neil. But I did not write.

Solemn days passed and nothing came; weeks passed and nothing came. The desire to hear from him became so overwhelming that it led me to dream strange and disturbing dreams of death and loss, in which my family were no more and there was no one left in the world to love me. These dreams so coloured the dismal atmosphere of my world that even the sun, streaming into my room seemed to mock me, and I shut it out.

But I had been looking for work and at last I was on my way for an interview for a job, but since the world had become such a grey and passionless place for me, and since the edges of my good nature had become so ragged, I found myself in shirty mood in the presence of the well-known and respected Mr Dallow, headmaster of a Gloucester school. He had the reputation of being the most popular Head in Gloucester and he was about to give me a grilling. He appeared stern when I met him and I was in no mood for a confrontation.

'Do you teach much nature study?' was one of his first questions.

I gave a rather starchy, 'No,' then regretted it and added, 'but I like it.'

Making an effort to be pleasant he said, 'You see, there is so much opportunity here for the study of wild life.'

This only increased my acerbity. 'I've been disappointed in what I've seen . .

. or haven't seen.'

Slightly taken aback and a little nettled, he responded, 'Well, I doubt if you've been observing your environment very carefully.'

'Not at all,' I said fearlessly, 'I'm sure I have. For example, there's a great lack of birdlife.'

After all, I had a passion for the natural world and I wasn't going to be told I was unobservant, but then again, he wasn't going to be upstaged by a young upstart like me. Argumentatively, I named all the birds I should have seen but hadn't, and he went on to contradict me.

But I soon sensed his good naturedness and he sensed the youth in me, and we soon dropped our mantle of crustiness and a twinkle in his eye did not escape me.

The interview continued, and he finally said, 'Really, Miss McKinlay, I should have ended this interview a while ago, but I am enjoying our conversation and I admire your candour.'

However, he had one more question to put to me.

He explained that I had satisfied him on every point so far but that his school had a high reputation for needlework, and he wished the standard to be maintained.

'Would you be willing to take needlework?'

'Oh, Mr Dallow, I'm so sorry, I can't sew.'

This took him greatly by surprise.

'But Miss McKinlay, *I* can sew!'

'It must be a great disappointment to you, Mr Dallow,' I said, 'but as soon as I lift a needle, everything goes wrong. Honestly!'

Still trying to persuade me, he continued, 'You see, my needlework teacher is leaving and I can't get anyone to take her place,' and he gave me a hopeful look.

'To tell you the truth, Mr Dallow,' I said, 'I can prove my point. Look.' I drew a button from my pocket. 'This button fell off my coat six weeks ago and it's still lying in my pocket and, what's more, I didn't even sew it on for this interview!'

Mr Dallow laughed. 'Miss McKinlay, you amaze me.'

The interview was over, but he went on to tell me how his sister had taught him to sew and how proud he had always been of his skill, and before I left, he entertained me with sketches of his childhood, and then he took me to see the school's conservatory and described his love of plants. By then I was shuffling awkwardly with embarrassment to think how petulant I had been at the beginning of my interview.

I failed to get the job, which was just as well for the reputation of the school, but we parted the best of friends.

Happy interludes of that kind perished quickly and winter moved on apace, until the gorgeous icy yellows gave way to the advance of spring, and by that time I'd received a teaching post in one of the deprived areas of Gloucester.

I suppose it kept my mind concentrated, bestowed some discipline on my day and provided me with money to spend as I wished. I travelled around and spent money on clothes. I had a difficult job because I was given a class of 'problem' children attempting to settle in this country from the West Indies. The job was not only difficult but it seemed impossible too. I could neither get the children to work, nor could I get them to understand what work was about. And since this was the case, I often had to resort to games in the playground, but when I did that, they ran away. They ran out of school and they hid in the toilets, and getting them together again was akin to rounding up wild horses. During lesson time, when I tried to elicit information they referred me helpfully to the headmaster. For example if I asked for the capital of England or the five times table, they would call out, 'Miss, just go to the headmaster; he'll tell you!'

There were little passages of fun supplied by my friendly colleagues slotted in between the stressful times. I remember telling Martin - a big, boisterous male teacher - that I was having problems.

'They just won't respond to me.'

'Won't they?'

'Sometimes I get desperate and even tell them things about my personal life, but they don't respond.'

'Don't they? What do you tell them?' he teased.

'Private things about myself.'

'And they don't listen,' his voice rang out.

'No.'

'Then tell me!' and we would all have a good laugh. I wouldn't have survived without their good humour and acceptance of me.

I think I pleased my headmaster, too, for he once told me how amused he was to hear these coloured children sing, 'The Bonnie Banks of Loch Lomond'.

So, school was fine, the money was fine, and Mrs Stone was fine. However, I still had many a sleepless night, which brought an unsettling nervousness when for example, the skies seemed to be forever blue when I yearned only for the rolling grey cloud of home. A big chestnut tree grew across the road from the house and each morning, as spring approached, the buds - big, fat and sticky and stretching upward to heaven's light - confronted me as a symbol of vulnerable love, rising, but doomed to be cut down.

One day, Mrs Stone caught me lingering by the small table at the bottom of the stairs.

'Are you all right, dear?'

'Yes,' I said, moving on. 'I was just hoping to get a letter.' I pretended a heedlessness.

'Are you expecting one?'

'Well, no . . . not really. I'm not sure, to be honest, but I was just hoping,' and I started to climb the stairs.

'Well, if anything comes for you it will be left on the table.' And, as she moved off into the family room she added, 'I hope it comes.'

Well, the vessel might be strong, but the spirit of the captain of the ship was wavering without his flotilla of helper ships. When a letter came one day from Mike wondering where his 'little star' was, and requesting her company which would be 'an inspiration' to him, this did not cheer me up, and I treated him much as a 'ship that passed in the night', keeping him strictly to the 'shipping lanes.' So, happiness that was offered and might have changed my life, perished in the bud.

But I made the most of exploring my environment, for just as I had trudged through the snow of winter to look at the county, now I explored the rustic villages as the cherry trees and apple trees were bursting into bloom. I found myself in cathedrals and abbeys, pondering the work of ages past, and watching the cricketers in fields.

The spring holidays were approaching and mamma came down to Gloucestershire, ostensibly to shop and do a bit of sightseeing, but in reality she had come to reassure herself about my situation, perhaps even rescue me should it be required.

I knew I didn't look too great, so I went out and bought myself a new outfit to 'paper over the cracks', and as I stood on the station platform waiting to welcome her, I fortified myself by remembering that I had not written to Neil in five long months, which gave a boost to my confidence.

During the day, as I was still teaching, she was left on her own to spend the day and later I was to discover she had been searching the city for signs of social activity that she might interest me in, for she knew I was not taking much part in life. On the day she returned home she had left a note on my table, with the address of a Quaker meeting house, and she suggested that I go along and make friends of these nice people, and in her thorough and painstaking way she'd even left a note of the days and times of their meetings.

One evening I went along to the Quaker meeting house and enjoyed it, being impressed with the kindness of everyone, so I continued to go for some time. On one occasion, when the meeting was over, I was invited along with a group for refreshments at one of the local pubs, and there I met a bachelor, Syd, and we struck up an instant friendship, which was to usher in for me what I was to describe as my 'Golden Age', for it combined the gold of the early summer sun and the gold of his deep, rich voice and the golden days of listening to the music he played for me.

Short and squat, fat-faced, red-cheeked and bald, Syd was not the stuff that dreams are made of, but his attitude to life – so positive, so unlike my own then – was at that time, a gift. When I awoke in the morning, it was to sigh at the dawn of another day, but when Syd awoke it was to welcome in the day with a smile, and relish every waking moment of it.

He occupied a room in a detached Victorian house in Heathville Road a broad and tree-lined street in Gloucester, and I soon became a regular visitor.

The first time I was invited to see his accommodation, I remember I exclaimed, 'For goodness' sake, Syd, what a shambles!'

'What do you mean, "What a shambles?"' he said, carefully stepping over various articles which had taken up residence on the floor.

'Well,' I said, looking round the room, 'you've got stuff everywhere!' and I made my way over, under and round about various articles towards the chair he offered me.

'I like it like this,' he said, gesticulating, as an actor does with an air of exaggerated drama. 'There's nothing wrong with the place!' he protested with a child's sense of fun.

'There's nothing *right* with the place!' I said, sensing the beginnings of pantomime.

He had a table which I never saw cleared of books and papers, except when he moved these aside for his dinner plate. One corner of the room was taken up with musical equipment, because music was the great love of his life. Piles of records were stacked against the wall, which they shared with a motley collection of fishing rods, walking sticks and photographic equipment. On a sideboard were more books and old guns and pistols. Occupying the floor space nearby was a cooker, stacks of plates, cups, saucers, teapot and kettle. Finally, in another corner was his bed, with only the legs visible, for it was hung generously with towels, clothing and bedding. But everything in the room was scrupulously clean, shining and fresh; a bit like Syd himself.

'Syd, you can't *move* in here and there's nowhere to put *anything*,' I protested. Whenever I complained he shut me up telling me to make myself a cup of tea.

'But I can't get near the kettle.' Teasing was part of the fun.

'Besides,' he would say, frowning at me like a schoolmaster to a naughty boy, 'I know where everything is.'

He had a way of dealing with me if I complained too much or sighed too

114

audibly. He'd stand still, look me straight in the eyes, raise a finger and frown, before saying, 'I've got something for you . . . come along . . . see this.'

He would then approach his music cabinet, choose a Haydn symphony and, with happy laughter, he'd put it on to play, rub his hands together and we'd both sit down and listen.

I had a lot of fun with Syd around a cultural life of music and reading, and often in the evenings he'd lecture to me on his favourite subject, history, his particular strength being the Roman era. He had a deep, well-modulated and polished voice, which was a pleasure to listen to. He would read me great chunks of prose from history books, and my interest was sometimes exaggerated and Syd, misinterpreting this for enthusiasm, would continue until my wearied lids closed in blessed relief.

He took me all over Gloucestershire and even into Wales on his Suzuki motorbike, visiting Roman sites of historical interest, and nothing was more exciting than racing through the wind, following the course of the Severn, and always favoured with, it seemed, summer sunshine, when the ancient churches, cathedrals and spires were lit with a radiance amidst the glorious golden fields of Gloucestershire in summer.

In return, I'd take him round the bookshops and buy him a book of his choice, introducing to him my favourite poets and writers, and when we sat in the garden under the apple trees, I amused him with snippets of family life, which always fascinated him, and we would talk the sun down the sky.

But Syd could discern that my quality of life was somehow impaired, and inevitably I revealed my relationship with Neil.

Seven months had now passed and I'd neither heard from Neil nor had I written, but nonetheless, on descending the stairs each morning my eye alighted on the little, empty table, which I walked past each day with a little stab of pain, and left the house, walking down the road pretending there was no such thing in the world as disappointment.

One morning in June, as I was leaving for school as usual, I looked on the table, so long a symbol of life and hope, and there lay a small envelope, but months of scrutiny and disappointment had become a habit, and I passed it by.

I was just turning the door handle when the unmistakably black, miniature handwriting registered on my brain and suspended life for a moment.

Yes! my brain said. *Neil's handwriting!*

I glanced back over my shoulder. It was not a mirage. My hand snatched it, my fingers fastening on the envelope. Time stood still. The letter was real!

'Mrs Stone!' I shouted. 'Mrs Stone!' I rushed into her room without knocking. 'My letter! It's come . . . the letter I told you about! It's come!'

I held it out. 'I knew he'd write. I knew it!' and I rushed from the house. I did not wait for Mrs Stone's response. I bolted! I tore the envelope open going down the road to school, but I soon regained my composure, as a wave of confidence surged through me. No need for all this haste I said to myself. *I've all the hours of evening.* I locked the treasure in a pocket and strode down the road. How lovely the chestnut tree looked! How lovely the flowers springing up. The sun streamed down, the clouds began to move and the wind began to blow. I gave my hair a pull. *This is real!* my heart sang.

But it was a special evening for me because, not only had I the priceless envelope in my hand, but also I could savour some sense of superiority, for it was I who had successfully withdrawn from the affair by not writing; I, who like a butterfly seeking flight, had kept her wings pinioned to the heavy, dull, unliving clay of earth.

But it was not the sort of letter I had expected. He said he had not written because there had been no good news to send me and that the previous Christmas his deadly, inert depression made him feel that he was on the verge of losing his sanity and he had been in hospital for three weeks. He had brooded a lot at home, he told me, and wondered if I was fighting fit or languishing sick, and ended rather sadly, 'I hope you've had a much better time than I, which your good qualities entitle you to expect. Even if you don't want to write to me, please let me know of any change of address.'

'Poor Neil!' I said to Syd, 'and to think of him languishing in hospital last Christmas.'

'My dear Eilidh, you must protect yourself from so much grief in your life and not let anguish burn your soul out.'

'But it's such a terrible irony, Syd, for I have always told him that if ever he was ill and needed me, I would always go to him, and to think that I have not been writing to him, believing him to be well and thriving.'

'I see what you mean,' said Syd sympathetically, 'but it's the method of self-help you've adopted, and from what you've told me of the past, I, a mere man, can only wonder at your enterprise.'

'Oh Syd,' I said sadly, 'if only he'd sent for me I would have gone. And now I don't know what to do.'

Syd had an old-world charm which showed in his use of language to me. 'Dear Eilidh,' he said, with much feeling, 'I feel distressed when you're unhappy, and I understand your need for a guide through this maze, but I fear I would fail in this territory of the heart.'

I said no more about it to Syd, but I sent Neil my address on a postcard.

It was at this time I moved house again, for Mrs Stone's newly married daughter required my room and, by an unexpected coincidence, I found myself living in the house next to Syd's. How Fortune smiled on me once more, for not only was I geographically close to Syd, and living in a street I dearly loved, but also I was an inhabitant of one of those spacious homes, that seemed forever solid and reassuring, a home of chiming clocks and polished wood. My room overlooked a sunny garden where my landlady, Miss Ellis, would play with her golden retriever dogs on many afternoons.

It was this new address I sent to Neil, and I also gave him Syd's.

Compassion was an emotion which, for me, dissolved all other feelings and considerations, so when Neil wrote by return asking if I would mind if he visited me, I returned immediately the peremptory, 'Come and oh, what joy!'

The following Friday arrived and, instead of going straight home from school, I went shopping and had a meal out. However, when I returned home, I found a note from Neil which informed me that he had called when I was out, but would return at five o'clock, but by then it was long after five.

In a panic, I raced to the railway station, but there was no sign of him. I then took a shortcut to the bus station but there was sign of him there either. Disappointed and dejected, I returned to Syd's, climbed the stairs, knocked on his door and went in, energy spent, and there, coolly eating strawberries, was Neil!

He seemed quite at home with Syd, and we three soon sat chatting about nothing in particular, but it was at times like these that Neil seemed relaxed and happy and free from sadness.

But now it was very late. I'd lost track of time and I wondered where Neil could spend the night for there was no room in Syd's. As I did not want my problem to be Syd's, or Neil's for that matter, and as the good Miss Ellis was spending the week-end away from home, I felt it could not be too harmful to take him into the room for the short night. I therefore slipped Neil into the house as unobtrusively as possible. After sharing a little of my supper with him I made a bed for us on the floor, and we lay there talking.

Many long dark months had passed since I'd last been with Neil; much water under the bridge, and many cheques into banks, and I felt under constraint not to say too much. But I wanted to get a feeling of how things stood between us, yet could see he was tired. Besides I had a dread of those intimate moments when, as often before, words had been spoken that shattered my fragile hopes, hopes which kept returning especially every time he came back to me. But I had to know. There was tension hanging in the still, quiet air of the night when words acquire an added strength. He whispered, 'Things haven't changed. You know you will have to find another, don't you?'

Once more the heart's shattered pieces fell away into the silence of the night, and once more the bell tolled my spiritual death.

Hearts broken or unbroken, one has to rise and breakfast, dress, and pretend to all the world that all is well. Neil left early in the morning and I accompanied him to Cheltenham.

I was unnerved and unsettled and glad to get back to the comfort and common sense of Syd and my passionless life.

'Oh, Syd!' I cried, 'I'll never write to him again. It's like erecting palaces of hope and deluding myself.'

'Yes,' said Syd kindly. 'I hope you won't feel it impertinent if I say that these "palaces" are built on flimsy foundations.'

I often felt a sense of humour that was wholly Syd's. 'Yes, it's like sowing seeds on rich fields and gathering in a poor harvest,' I said.

'And what you harvest is not enough to make it worthwhile,' Syd said.

'Hurricanes blow in and destroy what little there is,' I added.

Syd sat looking at me with a forlorn look. 'Was Neil not a little callous to have said what he did?'

'No, I don't think so, Syd. He says I attach too much importance to relationships. He once explained to me how he was different. He told me once of a deep feeling he had for one of his students, a French-Corsican. He felt he could have loved her if she would have let him. I remember he said she was flawed, in the same way he felt he was, but she sent him a letter ending everything, which for the duration of the evening and night tortured him with anger and bitterness. But by the next day he had forgotten her.'

Syd said, 'Eilidh, I have visions of you combating great problems and unhappiness.' 'And,' I interrupted, 'do you know something else, Syd? At times like this, when I'm on the point of leaving Neil forever, I recall something in literature, inadvertently, which encourages me to go on in this destructive way, almost as if Fate were an accomplice in this destruction. Can you believe that?'

'And have you found something like that?'

'Yes. I've been recalling the famous passage from *Wuthering Heights* where Cathy says to her nurse, of Heathcliffe, "He quite deserted! We separated! Who is to separate us, pray? Not as long as I live, Ellen. Every Linton on the face of the earth might melt into nothing before I could consent to forsake Heathcliffe! Oh, that's not what I intend . . . that's not what I mean."'

Syd listened and looked at me. 'Eilidh, I've not the humanity to do what you do. In some ways, you are Olympian, but beware of disaster.'

I thought for a moment before saying, 'The sad thing is, Syd, that I don't have the humanity you give me credit for. I have caused a lot of suffering to my family, who have loved me and stood by me and suffered for me, and I have quotations aplenty that would equally describe me most aptly. Listen to this from Henry James, and weep. "What I hate is myself when I think that one has to take so much out of the lives of others to be happy, and one isn't happy even then. One does it to cheat oneself and stop one's mouth but that is only, at best, for a little. The wretched self is always there, always making us somehow, fresh anxiety. What it comes to is this, that it is never a happiness at all to take. The only safe thing is to give. It's what plays you least false."'

Syd sat gloomily turning this over in his mind before saying, with a shake of his head, 'But I'm bewildered by your determination to continue. All I know is that I've always found a deep joy in living and I wish I could see you as happy.'

I think, for once, it was Syd who sighed.

'God knows, I bewilder myself. It's not that I haven't tried,' I said.

'As a counsellor, Eilidh,' he said, 'I can't be of much use to you, I'm afraid . . . but it seems strange the things that people will do.'

'And won't do.'

'What is it about Neil? What is this magnetism that draws you?' he asked, never taking his eyes from me.

I pulled my seat closer to the table where we sat and talked and he, opposite, crossed his arms in front of him, listening attentively and waiting.

'I've sometimes thought about this Syd, and it's not altogether easy to understand. I know it wasn't his scholarship that led me more deeply into the world of literature or poetry; nor the meteoric flame with which he lit up my world with brightness; nor was it his looks or background.' I paused for a moment because it seemed to me there were so many attributes that attracted me to him.

'You see, Syd,' I continued, 'my life has been spent in sunny pastures but the landscape that he seemed to come from was so bleak, melancholy and pessimistic that one would have perished on it. With his gifts and talents he should have been happy and had the world at his feet. But it wasn't like that. The nature of his intelligence set him apart and isolated him, and he seemed often to me like a lone planet in the universe, tracing its lonely trajectory. I think he struggled with this with humour and wit and tried to transmute much of this back "into life."'

I stopped and gazed across at Syd who still seemed to be interested, so I continued.

'Because I've thought so often about children in my career as a teacher, I've sometimes felt that Neil's childhood was not always happy. You see, when children are gifted and sensitive it often sets them apart and they are seen as being somehow "odd" and they don't always have an easy time. And it worries me too that he has had such a rigorous, intellectual training, which perhaps he ought not to have had, because his talents would ultimately have found their place. He wasn't happy at university, and often I think about that. But it's mainly speculation, Syd, at the moment.'

Having paused for a moment, I went on, 'Undoubtedly his personality played a large part . . . his humour, his intelligence . . .' My thoughts tapered off.

'Yes, truly you paint a bleak picture,' Syd said, 'and of course the fact that he was poor didn't help.'

Chin cupped in my hand, I looked at Syd waiting for him to say more.

'My dear Eilidh,' said he sadly but with a sneaking hint of humour, 'I understand your need for a philosopher to help you through this maze, but I feel my inadequacy profoundly, and as a guide, blindness I fear, renders me useless.' I was always moved by his antique way of expressing himself.

'But that's not all, Syd,' I said. 'You told me you were bewildered by my determination to continue, and it's this that frightens me most, and makes me think there is something strange about me to want to continue. All I know, by way of explanation, is that I've always had a deep sense of compassion, stronger than all other feelings I have ever known. I have always felt for wounded things, and any form of cruelty in this world takes a heavy toll of me. I've always seemed to have a need to protect things that might be harmed. It's just the way things have gone for me. I know it was compassion that was the binding force as the sadness in Neil's story unravelled.'

But I reminded Syd that I had not totally ruled out a life together for us, else why did he keep coming back to me.

Syd was staring again and shaking his head.

'Tell you what, Syd,' I said, seeing he had had enough of my troubles, and trying to brighten him up a little. 'You say you feel inadequate as a philosopher, but how about as a friend?'

'Oh, as a friend,' said he brightening up, 'I may do somewhat better because of my good intentions and my regard for you.'

'Well,' I concluded, 'I just want to see Neil happy, and it's hard for me to cease from an activity that's wholly good.'

'And *is* this wholly good?'

'I don't know.'

'And will you stop writing to him?'

'Would it make you happy if I did?'

'Yes. Would you stop?'

'Well, I could if I gave you my promise.'

'Do you promise, then?'

'I solemnly swear.'

The following day, while out shopping with Syd and when his back was turned, I dropped a letter into the postbox addressed to Neil!

But my conscience got the better of me and I told him.

He replied, 'Now I see how difficult it must be to reform a hardened criminal!'

My sojourn in England was coming to an end and it was almost time for me to return to my home in Scotland.

Syd begged me to stay. The headmaster promised me a job. My landlady promised me the room and mamma said I must do what made me most happy, but I decided to return home because my father was ill and my grandpa had just died.

One early Saturday morning, the phone rang and, as Miss Ellis my landlady was spending the week-end away from home, I answered it.

'May I come and see you?' It was Neil! I recognised his voice!

'Yes, if you want to.'

'Oh, don't say it like that,' pleaded the voice. 'Tell me you want me to come . . . oh, please tell me.'

'You didn't give me your name.'

'The Archbishop of Canterbury.'

'Oh, Neil,' I laughed, 'come as soon as you can and stay for as long as you can. Now don't waste precious time. I will expect the Archbishop very soon!'

I rushed out to the shops to buy some food for us, trying to stay calm in the circumstances, that is to say, that I'd soon be seeing the Archbishop.

Then I felt I was being followed. When I turned round, there was Neil, and we walked jauntily down the road together in the summer sun. I remember thinking how pretty I must have looked that day for I had just bought a pretty sleeveless cotton frock, and was wearing new multi-coloured sandals, such as summertime Gloucester calls forth to wear, so different from Highland summertimes.

Our arrival at the house coincided with the arrival of Syd on his motorbike, and I asked him to give Neil a ride on 'a real bike'.

Syd was happy to oblige, but Neil looked rather rigid as they moved off and Neil told me later he would have preferred a helmet.

They weren't away for long and when they returned we all sat in Syd's house and chatted in the most friendly way. Since Neil had been for a spin on Syd's bike, he recalled the time, to Syd, when he and I travelled between England and Scotland and were drenched with snow. With a look of pride on his face he said, 'I will never forget it, Syd. Eilidh's reaction was to laugh aloud.'

Anyway, I felt we were wasting the lovely sunshine of the day and I didn't want to embarrass Syd with too much of our company, and we soon left.

As we walked out into the sunshine on that happy Saturday afternoon, Neil told me his parents were going away for a holiday, and invited me to spend some days with him at his home. This was the first such invitation, and my heart raced. I might never get the chance again.

We walked hand in hand along the pavements where the crowds thinned and the pavements broadened.

'Would you like to come?' he put to me.

I breathed deeply, summoned my strength, and rather tersely replied, 'But that would not fit in with my plans.'

'But what is your plan?'

'I'm going home.'

'Are you?' he said, in a slight tone of defeat.

'Yes, and my seat is already booked on the bus.'

'But couldn't you cancel it?'

I could. It would be simple enough. I hadn't much time to cope with the temptation. I thought of mamma. She had said I must do what made me most happy.

I hesitated for a moment before saying calmly, 'Neil, I am going home.'

But I never knew how I resisted.

'All right,' he accepted, 'but when you get home will you write and tell me how you are, and whether you are coming back or not?'

I kissed my index finger and placed it on his lips.

We found ourselves strolling along the banks of the canal and on towards the fields, where we sat on the grass in the warm sunshine, then we lay and cuddled, not realising we were close to a railway line, and when a train passed, I sat up suddenly and, seeing the driver, gave him a wave.

'Shameless hussy!' said Neil, and the driver waved back!

Neil was relaxed and, as usual, always interesting, for my imagination was always pretty empty of ideas. We talked about this and that, and laughed about this and that, and somehow began talking about the use of language and the place of slang in teaching, and finally, obscenity. Neil wondered if I knew the exact meaning of four-letter words and I did not. One thing led to another and then he confided quite an intimate thing, and very revealing of his own curiosity that never seemed satisfied.

'I remember,' he said, 'I had accepted a lift in a lorry and, after travelling quite a long way, we came to some woods.' Here he paused for a moment. 'Then, for some obscure reason, the lorry driver seemed to get some mistaken impression of me, because he stopped the lorry and made signals for me to follow.'

Though I pressed him for more details he seemed reluctant to give them.

'You didn't go, Neil?'

'Yes, I did.'

'But why?' I was aghast.

'I was horrified by this, I can tell you, but I was curious and I wanted to see how far the man would go.'

'You went right into the woods with him?'

'I wanted to see what his next move would be.'

'Every step of the way?'

'Yes, I wanted to see how he would go about this.'

'And then what?' I asked, deeply shocked.

'I fled, but only at the last possible moment.'

'Really Neil, what risks you take,' I said, but I was glad he could talk of these things in the peace of the long, green grass.

After some more time had passed, I asked him if he would have tea with me.

'No, I'm afraid I can't. I must be getting away. My mother will be expecting me.'

I was a little disappointed, but I thought it was a curious thing that on our way back to the city we passed a restaurant and he suggested we go in after all. By the time we came out it was really getting late, and I offered to see him off on the bus home, but he insisted on coming back to my place where he stayed for another hour or so. I thought that, by then, he would have shown a little agitation at returning home so late, especially when his mother was expecting him.

Looking at my watch, I suddenly said, 'It's half past ten, Neil. You'll have to go if you want to get the last bus.' We started to hurry and soon bolted from the house, but he missed the last bus. We then dashed to the railway station, but he'd missed the last train too.

Out of breath by this time, I panted, 'Neil, I'll have to leave you and get back, or Miss Ellis will have locked me out.'

'I'll have to walk home,' he said with resignation. I felt sorry about it, but what could I do? He lived in Stroud, quite some distance away.

'It's a lovely starlit night,' he said with the beginnings of a smile. He gave me a kiss.

I watched him cross the road, thinking how silly it was to get into such a predicament, which could so easily have been avoided, as if somehow it had to be that way for him.

He looked back, saw me watching, rushed back across the road, gave me another kiss and disappeared into the night.

But I did not sleep that night because of something mind-blowing that Neil had said to me before we parted. He'd said, 'If you decide not to return to Gloucester, I'll come up to Scotland and have a holiday with you, perhaps in the autumn. I plan to work in London soon and if you are still "unattached", you could come to London too.' I was surprised but it gave me a new lease of life and, at the same time, caused me puzzlement.

My return home, however, was less successful than I had hoped. All the uncertainties of my life were dragging me down, and I now had to solve the problem of Mike because when I arrived home a letter was awaiting me which was an invitation to go on a Highland holiday with him.

Mike was easy-going and charming as well as being handsome, but I knew I was capable only of disappointing him. I'd already declined an invitation to go to Birmingham and meet his parents, and I'd previously told him that we could only be friends because my life was already distressed by intimate bonds of friendship with another. Since I had made all this clear to Mike, I felt all right to go because we had this understanding; but it turned out to be a fearful mistake, and a punishing time for Mike.

It was only when we were travelling north in the car that I was told we were going to Acheninver. He didn't know it would sink my heart like a stone. My memories were of the days when it seemed life was a paradise of fun and laughter and that the future held nothing but promise, hope, love and joy. Now that was all gone.

There in Acheninver I recalled my first walk with Neil. I looked on the mountains that had once stirred me with awe, and I felt empty, a stranger in an alien land. The mountains held no magic for me now but only reflected my solemnity and torture. It fairly immobilised and silenced me. I did not know it would be quite so bad.

When Mike took me for a walk over the moors, my true companion of the moors and mountain was not there. When I felt panic, I would rush away down the boulder-strewn moor, and only stop when I saw the sea again. Then I would stagger down the path to the old hostel, numb with anger at myself. When Mike returned I tried to make up for it by swimming in the sea with him and staying in for as long as I could.

From Acheninver Mike decided we were going to Craig which was, for me, another fearful disappointment and the choice surprised me, for Mike had found it uninspiring when we'd been there the summer before with Valerie. However, I knew Neil would not be there but would be arriving later.

As we drove along towards Craig, I glanced at Mike from time to time and was surprised that he was calm and comfortable and gave no indication that he was unhappy in any way.

Then I did a stupid thing. I asked Mike to let me out of the car to walk the last part of the road, which he did, but I didn't realise that it was going to be thirteen miles of steep and tortuous road that physically tore me apart.

But Mike was very kind and had left my wellingtons at the roadside when he parked the car, prior to the three mile journey over rough ground to Craig.

That evening, I accompanied Mike when he went strolling with his camera and he laughed to see the awesome scenery disappear in the time it took to get his camera out.

Returning later, a little wet from our stroll, I saw the figure of a young woman just disappearing into the hostel. All my senses suddenly fixed on the idea of this woman, in a strange mortification of soul. It was the return of the old jealousy, a quite alarming feeling.

I laid down my wet things and Mike went off to wash and change, and I was left alone except for the young woman who sat at one of the tables. She was a solitary figure. She compelled instant attention, for she was heavenly beautiful, her hair a swathe of gold, her face a map of peach and cream and she seemed to shine with an almost religious radiance.

All my senses fixed on her in a weird death of soul, for my jealous mind wove a web of imagined association between herself and Neil. She was here. Neil would be coming. I knew I had to do one thing . . . approach her and exorcise this devil within me or suffer hell. She must be confronted. I moved slowly closer, silently and steady as a rock. Would she have a deadly power to hurt me? In that one female form were contained all the attributes I lacked, all the strange, unknown and elusive qualities that would win his admiration and respect, all I'd coveted for so long. One talent after another would unfold and reveal itself. Timidly, fearfully, I descended on the hideous territory.

My halting reserve mellowed my tone and my fear to distraction gave an unearthly thistle-down to my voice, and my first words fell like softest down capturing her sympathy. In an instant I knew I had no rival.

Her name was Marilyn and she was with her boyfriend Tony, and I soon arranged for Tony and Mike to go off climbing, while she and I went off to Lochinver to shop, where I bought afternoon tea for us, and the rest of the day we walked, confided, laughed and shared secrets and parted, finally, the best of friends. They left the following day.

Mike decided to stay for one more night, but that extra night almost proved too much for me.

I will never forget that last night in Craig. There was no lamp in the upstairs bedroom which I shared with one solitary female who had arrived late that night and whom I had never met. In the darkest hour of night, I suddenly awoke from a deep sleep and, terrified, I sat bolt upright. It was black as pitch. There was no star in the sky, not the remotest twinkling. I was being buried. My heart raced. I jumped out of bed. I rummaged with trembling hands for the candle. I found it on the bedside table, together with the matches. I felt I would be trapped if I didn't hurry and light it. I lit it only to find there was just the merest trickle of light that seemed only to blacken the darkness even more.

Then it went out. I scrambled to the door. I had to get Mike. But how would I see him? Which bed was he in? My pulse was throbbing. What could he do, anyway? What about the girl in my room? I could wake her. But she would be frightened. Mike would be angry. I couldn't see to go out into the night. I jumped back into bed, pulled the covers over my head and, to the quick beating of my heart, I repeated mindless words over and over to the rhythm of my fast heart-beat, tapping with my hands and feet until I finally got to sleep.

The next morning the sun shone from a clear blue sky and the birds sang their sweetest songs. I walked out across the heathery ground, then ran down to the edge of the sea, where fresh winds blew in. The river gurgled happily, laughing in its song, and Craig seemed all at peace, even friendly as it showed off its charms like a peacock flaunting its plumes. I lingered a little longer and made my peace with Neil's spiritual home, which had been so unkind to me, but which now, in my own way, I had forgiven.

We left that same day after I'd seen the local doctor who gave me something to help me sleep. He was kind and indulgent, so that I left with a sense of much gratitude.

But we had to rush to Kyle for the dispensing of the prescription and Mike, who had now decided that he wanted to stay longer, became irritable and we had a row. However, he cheered up immensely when he discovered that the land he could see across the water was the island of Skye. We ended our holiday there, and I think Mike enjoyed himself and returned home revitalised, but at the end of the holiday he must have realised that I was not nearly so fine a person as he had at first believed. Our relationship had been doomed from the start, and though I often thought of him with tenderness and sorrow, I was never to see him again.

CHAPTER 13

Yet another phase in my life began when I took up a teaching post in Glasgow and found myself accommodated in a flat in Queen Margaret Drive, the home of Miss Purdon in the city's west end, near the Botanical Gardens. And Neil had gone to work in London, a new phase in *his* life.

The last time I'd seen him had been in Gloucester, and the things he'd told me then had remained locked fast in my mind, but I still proposed not to write but to get on with my new life, and found an outlet for my emotions by writing to Syd who had told me, not long before: 'Please remember that in writing to me you do not intrude, but rather you enrich my thoughts and feelings; and that you, to some extent, draw a mutual understanding from me so that when *you* are sad, *I* am sad, and when *you* are happy, *I* am happy. Remember what a student of Cicero said, "Friendship exceeds kinship."'

I had heard from Neil earlier telling me that his first story drew to a close and asked if I would like to read it. Of course I wanted to, but I didn't want to feel provoked into writing.

It was early winter.

The house was warm and my room amply furnished, with beautifully carved mahogany furniture and I loved the space and the comfort around me.

Miss Purdon, a middle-aged spinster, worked each afternoon for a charity, and when she returned each evening about five, she poured herself a glass of sherry but not before offering her little 'dear' a glass, which I never accepted for I never felt the need. Although we had our own private areas of the house, we saw a lot of each other for we were often in the kitchen cooking together or making coffee. She was strict, but kind, and on a cold winter's evening, she would invite me to have tea with her in her own private apartment. She took a great interest in me, thought I looked thin and careworn and eventually she found out about Neil and me.

But Neil's letters to me now took on a new expression. Change was afoot . . . a new spirit abroad . . . a renaissance? Letters and postcards came in fiery and neurotic floods, full-blooded, scribbled and full of assurances that he was thinking of me in the heart of a world capital. He had enough in his mind to fill dozens of letters, he told me. He would puzzle me sometimes. 'I'm at last sorting out and simplifying things,' he wrote. 'Nothing new, just the oldest and simplest in a new light.' Then there was the extravagant, 'You've been far more patient and suffering with me than I could ever have deserved. There's more to enjoy than we realised and the way is so simple.'

But the most exciting and memorable of all, and which I would recall over and over again: 'Come when the time is right, but don't come without warning.'

His happiness was irresistible, and he told me, with exuberance, that he'd just been reading about an eighty-year-old who had just been climbing the mountains between Melbourne and Sydney and who was looking for challengers.

'There will be a challenger if I'm still fit in fifty years time. What exultation when one's contemporaries were, like timid snails, withdrawing the horns of their endeavour and growing stiff and more crabbed and bent with every sunset. To be defying Time oneself and still shaking one's fist at the gods from mountain tops on one's eightieth birthday, and sleeping under hedges and trespassing and lighting fires, and penning savagely comic satires against wealth and power and principalities, and corrupting one's great-grandchildren with blasphemous and revolutionary notions about putting the pursuits of excellence and enjoyment before the preservation of their bank balance and the attainment of position. I can look forward almost to being eighty, divinely gay and irresponsible; guilt and dissatisfaction no longer a fruitful spur to mend the world or mend myself.'

I told him his exuberance was infectious and I was carried along on a high-flown tide of his energy. It was as if the tide were turning, and I took a risk by offering a daring suggestion. I said I'd share a flat with him to let him continue his writing. I went further. I even suggested he seek the company of other girls: 'Females of more exotic plumage than I, a common sparrow.'

However, some time later, when I mulled over what I had done, the 'cloud of thunder loured' at the mere thought of my impulsiveness, for I realised that, since I'd given him 'carte-blanche' to seek new girlfriends, he might consider sexual relations all right too.

I wrote feverishly and told him, in no unequivocal terms, that if he considered sexual relations all right then we were finished. I admitted that it was probably wrong of me, certainly selfish and ridiculous and a piece of dogma on my part, but whatever, it made no difference, and he was not to write again. And he did not write.

I took myself off for a week-end to visit Syd in Gloucester and on my return, found myself on the overnight bus to Glasgow.

At Liverpool the bus stopped to pick up passengers, which included a family of young children, as well as a gentleman in a pin-striped suit, not attached to the family.

It was a comment that Neil once made that I seemed to meet a lot of unattached men, and I was about to meet another.

I had slid down in the seat hoping to be as inconspicuous as possible, for I did not relish the prospect of boisterous children beside me for the journey through the night, and there was a vacant place beside me. However, the bus moved off and everyone settled down until a wailing rent the air, and this, apparently from one of the children who had been separated from the others.

I paid little attention until I felt myself being gently poked and, when I looked up, I saw the gentleman in the pin-striped suit asking if it would be all right if he could sit beside me. He had given up his seat so that the family could be together, which seemed a very decent thing to do.

I snuggled down with a soft moan to indicate as sensibly as I could that I wanted to sleep, for no one wishes to begin a conversation with a stranger which might last the whole night long, a possible burden of boredom. From a sly sidelong glance, I could tell from his expression, as he settled himself, that he was a very wide-awake gentleman. I angled my position slightly sideways from him, giving a tug to my cardigan round my shoulders. However, with his arms folded, and a smile playing around his mouth, he offered an explanation as to why the child might have cried aloud, which amazed me in its understanding of small children.

'You know,' he said quietly, 'sometimes in the heat of the night, a child's foot will swell and the strap of the child's shoe will tighten, and I think that's what might have happened.'

Well, he just *had* to be a nice man to have thought of such a thing, though nonetheless, I preferred not to be disturbed.

'Don't let me disturb you,' he apologised.

'It's all right,' I said and, attempting politeness, explained, 'I'm hoping to get some sleep because I've got to go straight from the bus in the morning to school.'

'Oh really,' he said, with my statement opening the conversation, at least for the first part of the journey. 'So you're a teacher?'

'Yes.'

'I tried teaching once, you know,' he whispered, 'but I wasn't suited to it.'

'Really.'

I was a bit irked at the start of a conversation which I had not anticipated so I felt that if conversation was about to be thrust upon me, then I would choose a subject close to my heart. 'My boyfriend's a teacher as well.'

'Oh, does he like it?'

'He finds it a strain, but he's good at it.'

He then asked if I'd been visiting my boyfriend and, since the subject of Syd would have bored me for the whole night long, I just told a lie because I was too tired to be bothered.

'Yes, I've been spending a week-end with him.'

'I've just been visiting a ladyfriend.' He'd clearly forgotten that I wanted to get some sleep. 'She's a writer, you know, but her greatest interest is poetry.'

'Really?' I said, with a shock of interest surging through me.

'Yes. She sends me her poetry to read sometimes.'

'You must have an interest in poetry too, then,' I said hastily.

'Yes. I'm interested in reading. I wrote a book, once.'

'You didn't!' I found the conversation livening up.

He explained that the book was not a novel, but a factual book about law in relation to industry, which did not sound very interesting to me, but it was the line of work Mr Bell – for by this time he had introduced himself as such – was interested in.

Proudly boasting, with no holds barred now, I told him that my boyfriend had just finished his first short story and I was soon to get to read it. He took so much interest in what I had to say that I felt quite ashamed of myself for lying to him earlier.

As I had some of Neil's writing with me – for I sometimes carried something to read – I asked him if he would care to read something Neil had just written. He showed interest so, after rummaging around in my bag, I pulled out something of interest and he read it. In the poor light of the bus, he read it again. After a pause, he gave an opinion.

'He's a very remarkable and evocative writer,' he said, then added, looking at me with a benign smile on his face, 'You know, reading this extract brings to mind all kinds of literary half-memories. Neil seems to take an unremarkable incident and make something valuable out of it. To some extent, it's a matter of combining the eager interest which children feel, with the reflective and comparative powers of the grown-up.'

I was surprised at his comments and, by then wide awake, I asked him again about his interest in literature.

'Well, you see, I studied literature at Cambridge under Dr Leavis.'

'That's a coincidence,' I said. 'So did Neil.'

I told him more about Neil and he said he wished he could be of some help to him in his writing, because he said he hoped Neil would find success. He had more surprises for me.

'Mine is an Honours degree in English Literature and perhaps I could act in some way as adviser. To prove my good intentions, and when I get home, I'll forward to you a reference which I was given by Dr Leavis when I left Cambridge.' And true to his promise that's exactly what he did.

But I made a decision to keep this surprise for Neil for some future time.

Mr Bell and I became good friends and he stayed near me in Glasgow's west end.

As for Neil, he had not replied to my last letter so that I could only conclude that it had been offensive to him in some way. The great flurry of correspondence had ceased.

'What a dismal afternoon,' said Miss Purdon as she passed me in the hall one late afternoon on her way to the kitchen. 'Are you all right dear?' she asked, taking a longer look at me.

My steps hesitated. 'I'm all right . . . thanks.'

'You look as if you have something on your mind,' she continued, her eyes following me. I moved towards my room.

'I'm just feeling a bit flat,' I answered, 'but I'll be fine.'

'Anything I can do, dear?' she kindly volunteered.

Turning towards her I said, 'I don't think so,' but, feeling the need to confide and the need for some help, and since I knew her good intentions, I added, 'but I think I've blundered with Neil . . . maybe I could tell you about it.'

'Yes, dear,' she said, moving into the kitchen, 'come and tell me what's happened.'

'Well,' I said, 'I really need your opinion. If I tell you what's happened, would you tell me honestly what you think. I'll respect your opinion.'

'Of course, dear.'

After putting her toast under the grill, she turned and faced me.

I told her what I'd written to Neil, about the possibility on his part of having sex with girlfriends, and that I could never stand for that; that it would be the end. I told her he had never replied.

'I tried to show a disinterested love, but I feel that I have lost him. I wonder, do you think I will ever hear from him again?'

She slowly sat down on the kitchen chair and shook her head. I didn't need to hear her words; she'd given me her answer, and I just walked away.

Mr Bell was my confidant by then.

'I've thrown a deadly dice,' I told him, and when I explained, he accused me angrily of arrogance.

'Do you really think a man would sign away his freedom?' I didn't answer. He could see I was hurt and followed this more kindly by saying, 'Really Eilidh, you must sink your pride in this matter. You must not be stubborn. Write at once to Neil. Write tonight.'

That night I gazed into a starry sky recalling the words of Housman:

'The rainy Pleiades wester,
And seek beyond the sea,
The head that I shall dream of
'And 'twill not dream of me.'

But I didn't write a thing. During winter week-ends I kept busy as Christmas approached by walking in the Trossachs with Mr Bell, brewing up tea and walking in the forests around Aberfoyle and Callander. And as I walked dreamily again around Deanston and by the river, where the trees used to heave in the winds, I recalled the earlier days when I walked and pondered the destiny of one for whom my hopes were as pure as the water that fed those trees, and an elusive sadness would bring nostalgia tapping gently on the windows of my mind.

Alone in the evenings I was drawn in memory again to the earliest days when we sported around the wilds of Ullapool, stretching our limbs over rocks and ledges, wandering the boulder-strewn shores, lochs and islands. Such memories of joy crowded in on me and I saw again a carnival of magnificent sights, sounds and colours; a distant and enchanting fantasia.

Whole centuries passed it seemed but he didn't write. Miss Purdon noticed.

'You seem sad, dear,' she said one evening in the kitchen.

'I'll be all right.'

'No letter today?'

'No.'

'You know you mustn't hope too much where Neil is concerned,' she said, with sharp insight. 'You know that, don't you?'

'Yes.'

'Maybe you'll have to forget Neil,' she continued.

'Maybe,' I knew no other word to say.

She came across to me and patted me on the cheek, saying, 'You're a dear little girl, but you do want me to be honest, don't you?'

I found it difficult to answer but, looking into her kind face I said, 'No, not really.'

Ten days later, I was sitting in school with my pupils watching an educational programme on television, when a note was passed to me from the headmaster, with the message that I was to get in touch right away with my landlady. I telephoned her and was told a letter from Neil awaited me.

My heart did not throb nor did my hand tremble, but in my soul sublime music played and I remembered something Neil once said:

'Kings cannot command,
Nor tyrannies destroy'
Such moments of life.'

That night I opened the letter.

He apologised for his long silence, which had been due to his characteristic disorder . . . depression with himself, with society and the general madness of the world. Hearing from me had been 'an undeserved pleasure'. He continued: 'Anyway, the silence does not arise from the possession of nubile, swarthy maidens from Istanbul or Freetown, from nocturnal rollicking with naked belly-dancers or any of the other very finite and so-soon exhausted resources of the flesh. Not a bit of it. I've led an utterly chaste life since we last held each other tight and kissed and caressed. I should tell you the truth, however much it hurts. Although I've given you sexual carte-blanche in the past and still do, this is not because I assume or require similar freedom in return or expect you to grant it because of such blackmail, nor is it to say that I don't respect your different point of view.'

I swallowed hard. What a man!

He continued: 'Perhaps if you met a man you were aroused by, and wanted to sleep with, I would not rebuke you. On the contrary, I would tease you with all sorts of indecently factual enquiries: Was he heavy? muscular? an animated hearth-rug? as bald as a coot? How did he plan and prepare and proceed with, and consummate his seduction?

Now I fear you'll be disgusted with me and I'm wishing you were here, lying on the bed, in a long tight embrace, with lips pressed together and our limbs entwined and our very breaths intermingling, instead of separated by 400 miles and a cold bleak night, and as unadorned as the day that we were born, despite your maidenly modesty and aversion to removing even the outermost of your 7 overcoats, skirts, sheaths, girdles, garters, bows, belts, padlocks, tights, slips, shifts and other preserves of virginity – the removal of all of which is, in itself, a triumph and a joy, though a frustration too.'

And my offer to share a flat had not gone unnoticed either.

'What you suggested was wonderfully kind and generous. Now that I have a regular job it could even work. It would only have worked earlier had I been quickly successful in raising money. To be kept by a rich patron is one thing; to be financed by the efforts of a hard-working friend, from love and faith, is another; and the burden of dependence of gratitude posed on the recipient could quickly sour the relationship. Now, as it happens, I'm receiving enough to support you too, if you felt like taking a year off the labours of instructing the young and not so innocent.

'In the event of such a household being established, London would perhaps not be the best venue. I'm pining quietly for the high hills and wild waters. Nothing can assuage that great longing but the hills and waters themselves. Glasgow is so close to the sea and the crags . . .'

This was the frolicsome Neil I knew.

He wanted to come to Scotland sometime after Christmas and wanted to holiday with me somewhere for a few days; he suggested a caravan perhaps at Fort William, but I was to choose. He left me to arrange whatever I wished.

Who could ever deserve such a boyfriend?

Some days afterwards, on my return from school, I found a note left by Miss Purdon to say that Neil had phoned and a letter was to follow.

In agitation, I waited for Miss Purdon's return. At the first sound of her step, I rushed to the door. She was shaking the rain from her umbrella. I grabbed it and bustled her in.

'What did he say, now . . . every word!'

Laughing softly to herself, she began unbuttoning her coat.

'Well dear, he said he had had a high fever.'

'More!'

'He said he wouldn't phone again today.'

'More . . . come on . . . what else?'

Trying to gather her wits while shaking the rain from her coat she continued, 'He said he might have to hitch a lift.'

'He's coming here?'

'Yes. He said that. He's leaving home on Saturday.'

'Here! On Saturday?'

'Yes dear, he said "Saturday".' Then she hung up her coat, closed the door of the cloakroom, and stood facing me, still not showing impatience. I stood in front of her, barring her way to the kitchen and knowing full well, on such a wet and miserable day, she would be anxious for her glass of sherry.

'What else did he say? Please tell me quickly.'

'That's about all dear,' and she moved past me to the kitchen, I following.

'Oh, Miss Purdon, he must have said more. Think!'

She now gave her attention to pouring her sherry. 'No, dear.'

'Well, did he sound happy?'

I could see that now she coveted her own privacy and as soon as she replied, 'Yes, he did,' I slumped into a chair.

She was just about to leave the kitchen when I jumped up saying, 'Oh, please, tell me it all over again!'

'Silly girl.' She smiled as she patted my cheek, put down her sherry and told me everything all over again, when I harassed her with questions, exclamations and interjections.

Then, laughing I rushed off to my room.

And the next day the parcel came, containing records of two Tchaikovsky symphonies, sent with love and 'thousands of kisses' and a 'six-hour hug'. An accompanying note told me he would be arriving five days before Christmas, that he'd be staying overnight, joining his friend Duncan for a spell of climbing and then he would return to me for the holiday that I had been allowed to plan.

New fires were kindled, warming my soul for days to come.

'I must hurry,' I said to myself, 'for he is coming.'

The day came soon enough and I chose to meet him in a scarlet winter dress. I sat in the stillness of the room with a full and glowing heart. My room shone as it had never shone before. Everything was in place; windows were opened wide to admit the fresh air, a fire glowed, vases were filled with flowers and cupboards were stocked with his favourite foods.

I wondered, as I sat there, at the *blitzkrieg* tactics of these last weeks. The bombardment of gifts, cards, letters when the door-bell rang.

I opened the door and there he stood . . . strange boy with the compelling power and magnetic pull that made me feel I was not complete without him. I couldn't speak.

'Oh, Eilidh, how well you look,' he said, with his warm smile.

I took him to my room, put my arms round him and hugged him, before he had time to throw his luggage down.

'I'll keep the six-hour hug till later,' I said.

'Really, Eilidh,' he said, 'you never seem to change. You always look so young and well.'

'You always say that, Neil, when you meet me, but you never seem to change either.'

I heard Miss Purdon's approach and knew she would be anxious to meet him. Unlike me, she was composed and I left them exchanging pleasantries, while I went to the kitchen to prepare the evening meal.

We dined in style at the huge dining table, with music in the background, and he sat hungrily and conscientiously eating his food, and I savouring every minute of this day.

I couldn't remember our having spent such a relaxing evening before, and we sat on the big sofa and warmed ourselves by a roaring fire.

I noticed a change in his behaviour in as much as he wrote a lot of the time, his notebook and pencil never far away.

He took me on an animated voyage through his most recent experiences, including his teaching ones and, when he saw me smiling he became more enthusiastic, and when his eyes met mine, he would smile in response, then continue.

He had often talked of his grandfather's cottage and I was always interested, for it was one of the few things ever mentioned that projected us into the future giving me cause to hope and to dream.

'Neil,' I said with enthusiasm, 'do you remember the little rowan tree I sent you once to plant in your grandfather's garden . . . the one I stole from the woods? Did you plant it?'

'Oh, yes, you sent me bulbs too. I looked after them in my own home until they were ready to plant and I'm expecting them to come up in spring.'

'Tomorrow,' I told him, 'I'm going to take you to the woods where I found that rowan tree. Would you like that?'

'I'd like that very much. You see, I desperately want to keep my grandfather's cottage; it's a place I love very much because I find such peace there.' His tone changed. 'I think I'll lose it, for there is some dry rot at the moment and I don't have money for the repairs.'

'Would it cost a lot?'

'Yes, hundreds of pounds. I've thought of all sorts of things that might work to keep it, but I just haven't been able to solve it.'

'I know it's your dream Neil, but there's no point in thinking about it if you can't save it.' Then, trying to be lighthearted, I added, 'I know what! Let's indulge in reverie and pretend we've lots of money to repair the cottage and you tell me all your plans for it.'

This was one of those occasions when he was very relaxed, as if he hadn't a care in the world, and he lit up a pipe and lay back on the sofa, and I, curled up at his feet, listened like a disciple to his master.

Of course he wanted the rustic simplicity of the cottage retained, the thatched roof and so on, but it surprised me to hear him say that he dreamed of having lots of children playing around, but did not mention children of his own, but children who had been orphaned. I heartily encouraged him. It wasn't lost on me either that he had begun his dreams using the pronoun 'I' but later changed it to 'we'.

Later that evening, when we were less serious, we simply indulged in horseplay, when he would chase me round the room. We'd fall on the floor and I would jump on his back and he would lift me off by the ankles and we generally behaved like young and irresponsible puppies, until the evening ended in an exchange of Christmas presents.

I then showed him to his room but did not stay with him, because Miss Purdon had graciously offered this hospitality, and if we were to abuse it, then it would have jeopardised Neil's chances of future accommodation.

But as dawn began to break I awoke just as the birds began to sing, and I rose and slipped furtively into his room, under the bedclothes and into his arms. But I knew only too well to be careful, for every floorboard in that old house had its distinctive creak, and I soon returned to my room.

For the next couple of hours, I lay in bed planning the day ahead for I'd promised him a day in the woods before he left to go climbing with Duncan, his long-time and much-loved friend.

I had to plan how far to walk with him, which forest track to take, decide at what time to leave and what I would take for the picnic.

I rose to prepare breakfast, while both he and my landlady slept. I dressed hastily, opened my door and peeped into the hall and stood listening, but could hear no sound from either bedroom. I padded quietly in slippered feet between kitchen and bedroom, but made not the slightest sound, apart from the occasional creak of the floorboards.

Just at the door of my room there was a little table, only big enough for the telephone to sit on with my address book beside it. That morning, however, I saw a small black leather-bound notebook, which did not belong to me. *Neil's!*

I stopped and looked. Strange how I stared. Strange how it seemed to stare back. A heavy stillness hung in the air. Strange suspension of life. Strange the magnetism of that small object. What dark power guided my hand, what compelling force? I hesitated. I mustn't. It would be wrong.

It was not the gentle touch of the benign thief, but the frenzied hand of one in panic that seized the book and attacked its contents. My eyes darted over the pages, sometimes seeing only in a blur, and then, with a restraining discipline I recognised titles of books, names of places, descriptions and even notes about meeting me, but what was I looking for? What made my hands tremble? My anxiety only increased because I knew there was something to fear. And I found it!

The blade of Fate ploughed deep.

I gently laid it down and stood like a rock in some dark place. Slowly my slippered feet shuffled into the room of Miss Purdon who was sitting up in bed that Sunday morning. Only the night before in that same room, I had shown off my presents from Neil and prattled gaily as a child.

Now I moved towards her, sat on the bed facing the wall opposite and for some time I did not move.

'What's gone wrong, dear?' she asked quietly.

One by one the tears splashed down.

Softly she said, 'Tell me about it.'

Tears dripped and dropped and I turned to look at her, and between sobs said that I'd seen copies of letters from Neil to two females, who had obviously been advertising themselves as 'grammar-school educated, intelligent, chess-playing females', and Neil's desire to meet them.

She spoke comfortingly as she always did to me. She let me cry out my sorrows and then she tried to rouse me.

'Now, dry your tears dear, and go down to the corner-shop and buy me my Sunday paper,' she said firmly, placing money in my hand.

I walked off as in a trance. I returned with her paper having noted the look of tenderness in the eyes of the vendor and the look of sympathy in the face of the street-sweeper as I passed.

In a mechanical way, I prepared the breakfast, for Neil was up and about. I scarcely even acknowledged him. I served the breakfast and started playing with my own. Then I rose from the table and sat by the fire alone, all my plans for that day turned to dust.

'Is there anything wrong?' he asked at last.

'I don't feel like eating,' was all I managed to say.

He wrote something in his diary and then continued with his breakfast.

To relieve the pain that was eating into me, I went to a drawer and took out a notebook and pen, sat down and began to write exactly how I was feeling, as one does in a diary to relieve the tension.

By then, there was an ominous silence in the room.

Just as Neil had finished his breakfast I said, 'I won't be going anywhere today,' which added to the ominous silence.

'Do you have to continue with that writing?' he said, with a hint of irritation. He must have wondered what was wrong.

I didn't answer but stopped writing except to underline a few words.

He began to collect some of his belongings.

'If you want to go anywhere today then you will have to go by yourself. I won't be leaving home.'

He came over and sat on the fireside chair opposite and once more wrote in his diary. This writing continued for almost an hour. He appeared not to be mystified by my behaviour.

When he closed his notebook I did not want to be in his line of vision, so I slipped down on to the rug at the fireside. He then surprised me by saying, 'When I return from my climbing holiday at Achnashellach do you think we could spend longer together in Perthshire?'

The caravan holiday I had arranged was at Dalguise in Perthshire. I said nothing for I was puzzled.

'What do you think?' he asked, with some urgency.

I still said nothing, but gave the fire a stir.

When I did not reply he asked if he could write to me when he was away.

I moved from the fireside to the table saying, 'There will be nothing to write about.'

'Well, I should be going then,' he said, standing there clearly realising that something was very wrong.

The minutes were ticking away and the tension mounting. I could hold back the unbearable pressure no longer.

I burst out, 'I read your diary this morning!'

He stood there, unperturbed and innocent and quietly said, 'That's all right.' There was no surprise. Unmoved, he added, 'There is nothing there but what is public.'

We stood there in silence.

My voice rose, 'I saw copies of letters to women friends!'

With the same calm and lack of surprise he said, 'But lots of people do that . . . I thought it was a good idea . . . it's lonely in the heart of a big city.'

It was said with such innocence that it made me seem a fool for making a fuss about nothing.

Icily I said, 'I've never done that!'

I saw him do something which I'd seen him do only once before and then only under great strain . . . he lifted his head and closed his eyes for a moment as if to shut out some hideous thought.

I moved over to the fire feeling a sense of puzzlement and a growing sense of bewilderment as if I was missing some piece of intelligence.

The silence dwarfed us in that big room.

Arm on the mantelpiece, I stared into the fire.

If my emotions had been less highly strung, and if my inner resources had been less bankrupt, then my thinking might just have been less addled and I might have recalled my giving him my blessing in seeking women friends, indeed encouraged him to do so, but I'd forgotten all that.

'I'd better go now, then,' he said sadly.

He lifted his bag and walked to the door, laid the bag down and turned to me.

'Have you any plans for next week-end?' he asked.

I gave a frosty 'No.'

I sat down again at the fireside realising I had a lot of things to sort out in my mind before his return if, indeed, I proposed to be there on his return.

'If it's all the same to you, Eilidh,' he said softly, 'I would like to come back from my trip a little earlier and spend longer with you. Maybe you would like to show me round Glasgow before we go to the caravan, but only if you would like that.' His words were spoken with great tenderness.

But I had not yet spent all my anger, and I had never, ever, at any time before, been angry with him, and in a voice rising with bitterness I said, 'If you want these "grammar-school educated chess-playing females" in your life then you can let me out of it.'

This remark made an unusually deep impact on him.

I rose to leave the room, but he came towards me and said tenderly, 'Eilidh, I'm sorry if I've made you unhappy. I worry about you because I feel you are too preoccupied with me.' His voice was sad.

'You see Eilidh,' he said, and surprisingly didn't remind me that the idea came from me, 'I'm so lonely in London sometimes that I feel a need for a friend.'

My emotions must indeed have been in turmoil, for even then I failed to have sympathy. With biting anger I said, 'If you just went out of my life, my unhappiness would end.'

He said not a single word. Then he sat down pulling me gently over to him and looked up into my face for what seemed an eternity, and strangely my fear seemed to vanish.

Then he took my hand tenderly in his and said, 'Eilidh, I don't think I could ever let you go. I'm so involved with you. I can't forget you. I have to see people I'm fond of. All my life I will want to see you. When I'm away from you I think of you all the time. Often I feel guilty because I think I've bored you or made you unhappy. All my life I should want to be near you.'

I rose in some agitation, my mind beginning to spin with all sorts of half-formed thoughts. I felt dazed as my mind tried to emerge from its state of blindness. I recalled all sorts of dimly perceived truths from the past. My thoughts were spinning and, in an effort to bring them back on course, I scarcely noticed that Neil was preparing to leave. I only knew he kissed me, and said he'd write and phone, and then he was gone!

I stood there for some time in a half trance, then moved slowly to my bed, pulled back the covers and lay, gazing at the ceiling and trying to clear my traumatised mind. I didn't move or sleep or eat, only my mind moved through labyrinthine passages of time and events, recalling everything that had happened in an effort to see the light. I never moved from my bed all day.

At last the fog lifted; the haze drifted away.

Neil loved me in his way. What did I want anyway? We'd walked together and talked together, we'd laughed and cried together. We'd slept together. His deepest thoughts, hopes and secrets were shared with me. I had his confidences. He wanted me, needed me and couldn't bear to be without me. What more was there to have?

The tangled web I'd woven began to unloosen as if by magic, and I saw through the lifting veil the dawn of a new day.

Come when the time is right rang out in my mind, and deep down I always knew there would be a time that was right and I knew the day would come and I knew this was the day.

And what a welcome he would get on his return.

And when he was away, he *did* write and he *did* phone and when he returned I was prepared. A huge fire burned in the hearth and the table was laden with food.

That evening we ate and talked. He described the weather, the climbs and the friends he had made. He told me he'd done a lot of writing, and offered me some for my opinion, which was great fun for me.

'And when are you coming to Glasgow, Neil?' I asked.

'And when are you coming to London?'

'Do you always answer a question with a question?' I asked.

'Are we going to Dalguise tomorrow?' he asked.

'Try and stop me!'

However, as it happened, we could only stay for a few days but I was excited about showing him all the places I loved, which he had never seen. 'I've been dreaming about it,' I told him.

The next day we set off in high spirits, travelling in comfort by train, chattering happily all the while, and myself so proud, showing off to everyone our togetherness, my arm tightly through his, whispering sweet nothings.

When we arrived a shroud of mist covered the countryside and the dampness caught in our throats and clung to our clothes as we walked.

'Oh, I'm so disappointed, Neil. I'd dreamed of showing you the sights,' I said with a sigh, as we approached an old bridge. I pulled him along. 'I've often stood on this ancient bridge on an autumn evening and looked up at the stars, and longed for the day when I could share it with you. I've seen so many beautiful moonscapes too, as I've stood here, but now there's nothing to be seen.'

'Don't be disappointed,' he said, moving his hand over the old mossy stone. 'Don't you see it's an excuse for coming back?'

I took him through the forest, thick with the smell of pine and, where the river intermingled with the forest, we sat down and watched the small ice-floes move along the river. When a biggish one sailed into view, I decided to tease him, for he was easily shocked – I jumped on to one and let it carry me along towards a treacherous current. When he called out to me not to be so reckless, I returned.

After a picnic in the forest when we used a tree stump for a table, we moved off again to the Falls of Braan, a spectacular waterfall, where Neil wanted to take a photograph and, foolhardy once again, I recklessly descended the slippery steps of rock, he following.

'It's not safe,' he called out to me. 'You should have an ice-axe,' his peace of mind threatened once again. 'Come back!'

With unheeding delight, I descended more quickly. In a letter to me much later, he described the terror he felt at that moment.

By evening, the damp and cold had increased and the mist fell more deeply.

We spent the evening in the caravan. We talked a lot and he wrote a lot, and tended to involve me by recalling from memory great chunks of prose of James Joyce, which I told him was incomprehensible to me.

'Incomprehensible to the experts too,' he said, 'for Joyce was a linguistic genius, who cared more for words than story.'

Midnight came and the stars were out and I took him for a walk in the cold starlit night, hand in hand, and we returned very late.

During our stay the weather didn't improve, but we walked and spent time in the small villages, and picnicked and let the time pass slowly. I couldn't remember a holiday that was more carefree, and, because of that, I didn't mind our return to Glasgow, nor even the fact that Neil would be returning to London again so soon, because I had such a package of happy memories.

We returned on a Sunday night and ate a hearty meal, but I insisted that Neil, and indeed both of us, go early to bed.

'I have school, Neil, and you know how the long journey tires you, so we'd better be well rested.'

In the morning he was up bright and early and full of nervous energy. Both of us bustled around feeling the strain that we always did at parting. We took a hurried breakfast and Neil gathered his things together, with an almost desperate excitement. We loathed partings. I put on my hat and coat.

'Don't go yet!' he said, fastening up one of his bags.

'I must or I'll be late!'

'It won't matter if you're late for once.'

My perceptions were razor-sharp at times like this.

'Don't write to me for about two weeks,' he said.

'But I want to write,' I insisted.

'And I *want* you to write, Eilidh, but I've so much to do at the moment I won't have time to reply and you'll be so disappointed. You'll make me feel guilty.'

'O.K. Neil, that's all right with me.'

'But don't worry, I'll write to you as soon as I get home.'

'Great!' I said, as I lifted my bag and looked at my watch.

Then we got ourselves into the strangest of parting conversations, for Neil was always full of surprises, often to my doom, in the past.

'Eilidh,' he said tenderly, drawing me close to him, 'you know many other people could make you happier than I.' I moved slowly away and sat down. He came and sat beside me. 'I so much want you to be happy. You know that, don't you?'

In the past, these little parting conversations terrified, vexed and distressed me; but not any more.

'Yes, I know that Neil,' I said, smiling with an inner sense of triumph.

His gaze was intent as he continued, 'Eilidh, if you married me there would be long separations.'

I returned his intense gaze and said bravely, 'I would marry you Neil even if I did not see you for months.'

'But you would be wondering what I was doing when I was away.'

'Not any more.'

I looked into his earnest face and knew how much he wanted to please me, but I would not want a commitment for he was still finding his feet.

'My complexities would hurt you, Eilidh,' he said in a soft, sad voice.

'I know them well enough.'

'You know I have a nervous predisposition which is inherited,' he said, 'and perhaps I would pass that on to my children, and I don't know if I could bear to do that,' he told me. I listened with growing understanding.

'You see, Eilidh,' he spoke quietly now, 'I have always felt that I should marry someone who was flawed like myself. I have always believed that. If I were to marry someone flawed like myself then, if I hurt her, she would hurt me and it would be an equal relationship.'

Although it was all so unspeakably sad I felt happier than I had ever felt before.

'I would not want you to get married, Eilidh, but if you decided to marry someone else, I would not hold it against you.'

Then, regrettably, I said something which should not have been said.

143

'How would you feel if I married someone else and never saw you again?'

He gave me such a look of despairing pain, that it stopped me dead in my tracks.

After a pause, when he seemed to gather himself, he said slowly and deliberately, 'Eilidh, I have to see people I am fond of. I've told you that before. I feel that about you more than about anyone else. Even if you were to kick and revile me, I would prefer anything to not seeing you, and I mean that . . . even to death.'

I was so touched and moved that Time seemed to stand still until the clock chimed out disturbing my reverie, and I jumped.

'I mustn't miss the school bus Neil,' I said, throwing on my coat. We grabbed our bags and ran.

'We never seem to have enough time together,' said Neil, before kissing me good-bye, and as I made my abrupt way to the bus, he ran off.

'I'll write!' I called, and we were swallowed up into the morning.

The great sea-change had come. The old, worn-out mantle of doubts and fearfulness was sloughing off and my new-found strengths were growing. I had kept secrets from him in order to surprise him. My friendships, conversations and my correspondence with Mr Bell I was keeping in reserve. And I had gone to university evening-class and had had some discussions with Dr Hobsbawn about Neil's work. But I was hoarding my treasures like a miser with his gold. However, I did not keep from him the address of a literary agent which I'd found in the pages of the *New Statesman*.'

And I had finally conquered the great destroyer, Jealousy, for though she had gorged on me, she had never destroyed the best that was in me.

And then began to pass the happiest few months of all and as I worked through them I feasted on all the good times we had ever had and all the nice things he had ever said. Only the positive things I focused my mind on. Then he wrote describing the many images that remained in his mind of our last holiday together at Dalguise, which caused him to comment: 'What a crowd of memories shared with you. What wastes of sand between these strung-out landmarks. Do you feel drawn that way too? Not a constant banquet or sequence of lush meadows, but a prevailing aridity and featurelessness interspersed with spots of joy, peacock hues, flashes of wings and precious stones, as rare as they are priceless.'

And I sent him a letter in return, but not like any letter I had ever written before, for I made it a landmark in my life because I wanted my love for him to be something rich and rare.

'Anything I have now or in the time to come, will be yours to share. You will never be without a place of rest, for my home will be your home, and you shall have it and all that it contains for as long as you may need it, and if you wish to be alone there, then that's how it will be. While I have anything, you need not want; never fail to ask and remember what I've said. In times of stress and illness there will be one friend who will not desert you, who will be forever the same, unchanging in her tenderness, never failing in sympathy, never wavering in her love, and there will always be a refuge in a strife-torn world.

'I will not be selfish about your future, Neil, for if you wish liaisons with women, then you must go out and seek them. Our friendship is secure forever, and I will be close to you in love and friendship for a lifetime. Nothing you have ever done has made me doubt your manhood or humanity.'

He wrote saying he was yearning for me with tenderness, that he was well-established now in school and had no intention of writing again to girls, and asked me to make tentative enquiries about teaching posts in Glasgow. Finally, he wondered when we were going to meet again.

I made preparations for Easter which was fast approaching and my plan, since Neil wanted to spend a few days climbing in the North-West, was to holiday with my parents at Dalguise for some days, and then rendezvous in Glasgow with Neil, spending the remainder of the holiday with him. Neil found the proposal 'excellent'.

Winter had almost drawn to a close. During the long, winter evenings, I had turned over many things in my mind and had finally resolved the way forward. It was, I suppose, what Neil had once described as 'just the old and simple things seen in a new light'.

A long and arduous journey had come to its unheroic end, but that journey had been travelled on a road, old and well-worn, but the road ahead was a new one, and the journey of this pilgrim only beginning.

The tide was about to turn, a new day to dawn and my time to come.

Everything went according to plan. Neil left to climb in the Highlands and I joined my parents in Perthshire.

These few days without Neil seemed endless, yet I was happy as never before.

On my last day, a fresh layer of snow had fallen overnight and field, forest and hill became a fairyland, whose beauty challenged me to be part of it. I threw my camera over my shoulder and went out to meet it. I ploughed my virgin way through the picturesque hills, as flocks of sheep strayed before me in scenes quite tearfully beautiful. I took many photographs.

'Wait till Neil sees these,' was the thought I revelled in.

And when it was time to return, I took one long, last look over the arctic scene and photographed it, but not before I gazed towards the mountains of the north, to where Neil was, and the skies then seemed lit with a warmer, golden glow.

I returned light of heart and light of step, softly singing to myself as the snow crackled underfoot.

But I was never to see Neil again. Unknown to me, while I walked over the hills that snowy day, with flocks of sheep straying before me, Neil had been climbing in the mountains that he loved, and had fallen to his death.

Shade and shadow fell upon my new road, so early in my journey, which now led to the valley of Loss.

It was the Easter of '65 on the moors of my homeland that I met him; it was the Easter of '70 on the mountains of my homeland that I lost him.

I was born with a capacity for love and compassion and suffering and I tried to use my gift for him, that he might use his gift for Art. I tried to stretch my gentle nature to contain the pain.

If sometimes you hurt me, Neil, then I have forgotten. If you should seek forgiveness then I should say, 'No cause, no cause'. If you are at peace now, then I could ask no more.

The flowers and the fruits of the earth seemed to perish, but the reality of his warmth, his gentleness and honesty did not die.

I said farewell on the wild path to the mountain where he died. Light mist hovered around the jagged peaks, aloof and austere, just the way he liked them. I stopped and listened to the moan of the wind that seemed to carry a forlorn cry, and I gently dried my tears.

Drops of rain reposed upon the flowers of the grasses and I bent and picked a few, kissed each small and dainty stalk, and laid them on the mountain of his death.

He would not hear the soft sough of the wind nor feel the little rain.

Old layers of Time's dust have lain upon my feelings for him, but have neither tarnished nor diminished them. They return now, no longer with a sigh, but fresh still, as they rise once more from slumber.

And now, each little pearl of memory falls quietly back into its fairy cradle, the going of each as gentle as its coming.

And the dialogue of life goes on and

> 'The clouds pass
> And the rain does its work,
> And all individual beings
> Flow into their forms.'